FEAR OF STRANGERS

iUniverse books may be ordered through booksellers or by contacting:

iUniverse
1663 Liberty Drive
Bloomington, IN 47403
www.iuniverse.com
1-800-Authors (1-800-288-4677)

ISBN: 978-1-4401-5918-3 (sc)
ISBN: 978-1-4401-5919-0 (ebook)
ISBN: 978-1-4401-5920-6 (hc)

Printed in the United States of America

iUniverse rev. date: 9/2/2009

FACTUAL HISTORICAL BACKGROUND

GEORGIA STATE CAPITAL, 1829

In 1829 a letter from Georgia's Governor Gilmer to the President of the USA charged the "Indian Nation of Cherokees" with violation of Georgia's sovereignty. He demanded that the Cherokees dissolve their local governments, renounce their claim to territory within Georgia's state lines, and move to land west of the Mississippi, land selected by the Federal government, not by them. Because the Cherokee Nation had allied itself with the British during the Revolutionary War, feelings among White homesteaders were bitter to all of them. Frontiersmen in the north Georgia regions seldom lost an opportunity to do harm to the hated "Indians" whose land they coveted.

WASHINGTON, D.C., 1830

On May 28, 1830 the U.S. Congress passed the Indian Removal Act. Shortly thereafter, Andrew Jackson (known as "Old Hickory"), the first frontier American President and the leading proponent for Indian relocation, signed the Act into law. He hypocritically announced this law for Cherokee removal would protect them from White encroachment since they'd be in a new territory and therefore free to perpetuate their race and their customs.

Even one of Jackson's fiercest political opponents, Henry Clay of Kentucky, applauded the new law, arguing that Indians were inferior to Whites and that their extinction would be no loss to the growth of the new nation.

CHEROKEE TREATY AT NEW ECHOTA, GEORGIA, 1835

In December 1835 Cherokee leaders reluctantly signed the Treaty of New Echota in which they relinquished their land in what is today north Georgia, south eastern Tennessee, and part of western North Carolina. They agreed to move to wilderness land west of the Mississippi. By means of a government sponsored lottery their now vacant land was sold to white colonists. Thus, hardy Caucasian pioneer settlers could later honestly and proudly say they purchased the land on which they began to build cabins, barns and raise crops and families.

CHEROKEE "TRAIL OF TEARS", 1837

The U.S. Military was assigned the task of rounding up all Cherokees into regional stockades and thereafter forcefully marching them to their new territory west of the Mississippi.

In 1837, at the end of Jackson's presidency, his administration announced that 46,000 Indians had been rounded up and removed to Eastern Oklahoma. In other records the number was as high as 100,000. No one really knew.

Reliable government documents reveal about 4,000 Cherokees died walking that 900 mile westward winter journey in what later became known as, "The Trail of Tears."

MODERN CHEROKEE RESERVATION

A few Cherokees, however, had managed to slip through the military dragnets in the Cherokee Round-up. They managed to hide in the nearly impenetrable mountains and forests in what is today known as western North Carolina. There ensconced, they endured decades of extreme hardships living in caves and temporary shelters.

Eventually a kinder Federal government ceded a large mountainous region in south western North Carolina to become "The Eastern Cherokee Reservation" or "Qualla Reservation." It occupies about fifty-five thousand acres. At the end of the 20th century within this sanctuary on their official rolls there were about 5,000 Native Americans.

Today, in the heart of this Cherokee Reservation, there's a large casino catering to "outsiders" whose gambling losses provide each living Cherokee a yearly <u>unearned</u> income of about $30,000, plus giving employment to all Cherokees who desire an additional generous wage.

This story is dedicated to all those honest men and women who struggle to overcome addictions...those who "lean not unto their own understanding"...those who "trust in the Lord with all their heart."

(Proverbs 3:7, Revelation 2:7, NASV)

PREFACE
"GHOSTS"

Clermont is a fictional town in fictional Clermont County. In this fabricated story both are located in northern Georgia. The town has a population of 2,010. In the entire County there are approximately 10,000 inhabitants.

The U.S. Forestry Service estimates there are at least 17,000 deer and 3,600 bears in their jurisdiction. Sixty percent of the land in Clermont County belongs to the U.S. Forestry Department. Another ten percent is owned by a State regulated Electric Power Corporation. Realtors constantly complain there isn't much remaining property for them to sell. That, of course, is the reason many outsiders who can afford to purchase home sites move to the region, a guarantee the area will always remain more or less a pristine wilderness.

In the late 18th century, after the American Revolution, the region was settled by hardy pioneers following the great westward expansion. The fledgling federal government granted Revolutionary War veterans wilderness land in exchange for their military service. It didn't bother politicians they were giving away land they didn't own.

For previous centuries this land at the southern end of the

Appalachian Mountain chain had been occupied by a race of people known as the Cherokee Nation, an agrarian culture Caucasian pioneers mislabeled "Indians," or "Savages," or "Pagans." Hardy Scotch-Irish and German settlers believed these native Americans were a substandard human specie, devoid of a soul, impossible to civilize, less intelligent than the wolves, bears, mountain lions, and deer that roamed freely throughout the region's fertile valleys and surrounding mountains. These "Red People" who possessed few guns were either shot, or exploited by White Man's whiskey, or infected and died by his contagious diseases for which they had no natural immunity.

In those early days, it was not uncommon for Caucasian pioneer men to marry Cherokee women. These mixed-blooded couples tended to be looked down upon by both cultures as the wives succumbed to the ways of their White husbands. Full-blooded Cherokees tended to cling tenaciously to old tribal customs. Thus they further became enemies of ever encroaching White pioneer settlers.

In the first quarter of the nineteenth century the Georgia General Assembly created the County in which the tiny settlement of Clermont was located, 960 square miles of undisturbed virgin timberland, fertile valleys, and an unlimited source of crystal clear mountain spring water. It was a magnificent unspoiled wilderness containing fish-filled rivers, spectacular water falls, and a formidable mountain range. It's an interesting ironic twist that to this present day many names of major boundaries, along with names of regional national forests and countless water falls have Cherokee names. Perhaps this state of mind in retaining Native American names for landmarks was caused by the subliminal guilt of those early homesteaders who literally stole land from its inhabitants.

What they'd done to the Cherokees remained a thorn in their psyche, a mental twinge of conscience passed from one generation to the next, a xenophobic knee-jerk reaction to all outsiders presumed guilty of trying to take from the "locals" what they'd forcefully taken from the Cherokees.

Those "from off" (the modern phrase the establishment gives to all not born within the County) who purchase a home in the region quickly sense this parochial paranoia. New comers are often told by local realtors, most of whom have their roots generations deep in the community, that in the entire Country live no more than 46 "Blacks" and only two Jews. The next piece of advice is that out-of-state new residents should quickly get Georgia automobile license plates because outsiders are dealt with differently than locals who have a preferred status. New residents soon discover, however, that the term "local" has many layers of meaning and is a moniker they can never claim.

Lingering in the valleys of the County are accusing Cherokee ghosts, cursing those who now occupy their land. These phantoms of the past sit just off the major highway bisecting Clermont County. If one carefully listens, they can be heard shrieking in laughter as they watch countless busses loaded with tourists passing through the County on their way to nearby western North Carolina and the mountain lair where opulent Cherokee casinos are located. These ghosts say "Amen" to the White man's God who said, "Vengeance is Mine. I will repay." The displaced native Americans are having their revenge. They gloat as visitors throw millions of dollars into the bank accounts of the "Indians" who three generations earlier were not considered intelligent enough to occupy this land.

In fairness, it needs to be said that a few descendants of those early Caucasian frontiersmen have managed to overcome this Cherokee curse. But fear of strangers remains ingrained in those mountain folk not inclined to trust outsiders.

Perhaps, just perhaps mind you, the only way to eradicate

CHAPTER 1
CLERMONT COUNTY, CIRCA 1940

"Shall I fill it up, Reverend?" asked Sam Smith, owner of the only gas station in Clermont County.

"Yes, please. Don't mind my son. He likes automobiles. This is the first car we've owned." The preacher's nine year old son was standing close beside Sam on the cement drive way as Sam had the nozzle of the gasoline hose pushed into the circular opening located at the left rear of the preacher's used 1932 Dodge six cylinder four-door black sedan.

"Likes to watch gasoline flow into the tank," said his father. "He's a curious kid."

"No problem, Reverend. I got a ten year old boy and he's always taking apart clocks, lawnmowers, toasters, and anything else mechanical. Curiosity's a sign of intelligence, they say."

There weren't more than two hundred automobiles in Clermont County. The town's doctor owned a new Buick Roadmaster. Reverend Owens of the big First Baptist Church owned this old Dodge sedan. Bill Brady, president of the one and only bank in the country owned a new big eight cylinder Cadillac. And, of course, the circuit judge owned a Buick. A few wealthy building contractors plus the owner

1

of the county's only hardware owned automobiles. Several carpenters, masonry workers, and heavy equipment operators owned trucks that were replacing mule drawn wagons. One gas station within the county was enough.

Reverend Owens entered the small office of Smith's Texaco service station two buildings south of the Clermont Café. He was looking above the door at a rack of tires when Sam walked in, stepped behind the counter in which his cash drawer was located. "That'll be a dollar eighty-nine Reverend. The tank took ten gallons." As he spoke, Sam was glancing out the front glass window at the preacher's son whose head was bent over the gas tank opening, chrome gas cap grasped tightly in hand, peering down into the now filled fuel tank.

"That kid of yours done got his nose right over the opening to that tank. Think the fumes might hurt him?"

Ignoring his question, the Reverend gave the station's owner a serious look as he handed him the price of the fuel. "Sam, guess you heard I've resigned my pulpit and will be taking my family to the Philippines to do missionary work?"

"No. I ain't heard that." Sam was obviously surprised and a bit disappointed. After making change for the preacher's five dollar payment for the gasoline, he looked up, asked, "Why do you want to leave us here in Clermont? Why go to a place where natives might want to kill you?"

"Sam, if you saw ten men carrying a long heavy log, and at one end there were nine men lifting and at the other end only one man was struggling to lift it, and if you wanted to help carry the log, at which end would you go?"

"I guess I'd go to the end where there was only one man."

"That's the reason I'm going to a remote part of the Philippines. Here in Clermont County there are at least fifty preachers carrying the gospel to those already saved. I'm going where there are few preachers and millions of unsaved."

Sam looked down, then with a gaze of admiration, replied, "We'll sure miss you and your wife and Tom."

There was another long pause as Sam walked away from behind his cash register, walked over to the plate glass window at the front of his station, looked out at the preacher's car next to the gas pump. "That sandy-haired son of yours was born the same year as my son Billy. Your son and my Billy are best buddies. Billy will miss him."

There was an emotional pause between them. Sam looked up, his voice resonating disappointment. "When you leaving?"

"End of next month. We'll be staying in the parsonage 'till the deacons find my replacement. Then, first of November, God willing, we'll be taking a steam ship from San Francisco to Manila. The Convention has appointed me to teach Filipino pastors in a seminary located in a city named Baguio. It's up in the mountains about 200 miles north of Manila on the big island of Luzon. I plan to dedicate the remainder of my life to that mission." He paused and then added, "I hope my boy can adjust to the new environment. Not too far from the mission in Baguio are mountain tribes of head-hunters and cannibals. Tom thinks of Clermont as his home since he was born here in Memorial Hospital when I was then preaching at the smaller Good Shepherd Church in Fruit Jar Junction."

"We'll surely miss your preaching," said Sam, his voice choking. "You've been a blessing to me and my wife Laura. Each of my six kids found the Lord in the years you've been our preacher. Yep, we'll miss you, but we'll be praying for you as you go to the Philippines to spread the gospel message there." He paused and then added, "There's talk that Japan is going to invade the Philippines. Aren't you afraid to go there?"

"No. Our Navy and army will keep that from happening." There was a long pause between them as Bill Owens pocketed the change from the five dollar bill he'd given Sam.

"Look at my boy out there. Looks like the fumes from that gas tank made him light headed."

Tommy Owens had stepped away from the car's left rear fender, had dropped the shiny chrome gas tank cap onto the cement pavement, was now sitting on the driveway curb, starry-eyed, his lower jaw drooping, his brain in a euphoric buzz.

No one thought much about it at that time. Years later Sam would recall this seemingly insignificant event.

CHAPTER 2
BALTIMORE, MARYLAND,
MAY, 1955

"You bastard! You didn't tell me you had a venereal disease?" Fire in her eyes, she added, "Now you've probably passed it on to me." She picked up a vase from the bedroom nightstand, hurled it. He dodged. It struck the wall and broke into many large and small pieces that littered the thick sky-blue carpeted floor.

With a gloating look on his face he said, "Why should I have it all to myself?" Steven Hurst didn't know which of the many women with whom he'd had sexual relationships had implanted this dreaded bacterium into the soft tissues of his sexual organ and into his blood stream. Hidden within his psyche was a contradiction: he hated all women, yet sexually desired every woman he could conquer.

His psychological problem was much deeper than having acquired a venereal disease. As an attorney, he knew what "misogyny" meant, but was in denial about being a misogynist. Spreading this contagious illness into as many women as possible was a form of subconscious revenge, retaliation for what he'd seen his hedonistic erotic mother do to his deeply religious father who'd once studied for the priesthood, a father he idolized.

As he glared at her, his eyes were threatening. She realized she'd made a big mistake when she came to live in his house. Young and naive, for the first time she understood that promiscuous sex could have dire consequences. She remembered textbook photographs in her high school hygiene class of disfigured prostitutes, dying women living in the last stage of syphilis. She shuddered at the thought of someday looking like them.

"You damn son-of-a-bitch. You knew you had it, didn't tell me." Again, she picked up another glass vase from the vanity table, threw it. This time he was not looking. The vase hit him on the left shoulder before falling to the floor and shattering.

Experiencing pain, he stepped over to the night table beside the bed, pulled opened a drawer, withdrew a pistol and aimed it in her direction. He wanted to kill her, but was afraid of the consequences in his pursuit of a career in the Democratic Party. Since acquiring this disease his future was already on hold. His dream of someday becoming governor would be totally ruined if he murdered his mistress. To frighten her, he aimed at the floor beneath her, pulled the trigger. The explosive sound panicked her. She bolted into the large dark walk-in closet, slammed shut the louvered door, crouched behind and beneath a group of dresses and coats. Out in the bedroom she could hear him throwing things, smashing perfume bottles on her makeup table. He was angry not just at her but at the world. He was a respected Maryland State Senator with a diminishing political future.

She heard him randomly firing the pistol at bedroom objects. She heard the large mirror on the wall crash to the floor. Would he next open the closet door and kill her? She too was angry, angry at him for exposing her to this disease. But for the moment her anger was defensive. She heard the pistol firing pin click. The gun was empty. Would he enter the closet, pull her out into the bedroom and beat her, bloody her beautiful face? Fear kept her crouching in the darkness, waiting.

Their brief life together had not been a happy relationship. Two months earlier they'd met in a hotel bar opposite the Maryland State capital building. It was the place where, after daily legislative sessions, State lawmakers gathered, made deals, received payoffs from lobbyists. She was an eighteen year old run-away. Not that she was a tramp, not at all. Her father was wealthy, had inherited immense riches from his parents whose blue-blood ancestral line dated back to a colonial ship tycoon who during the Revolutionary War had made a fortune smuggling arms and ammunition from Europe. Back then smuggling was a legitimate and patriotic enterprise. After the colonies won their freedom, her grandfather had established a firearm manufacturing company and sold his products throughout the world. In her family, shooting firearms ranked just below eating and sleeping. Her father never gave any of his precious time to raising his only child. He had, however, seen to it that expert riflemen tutored her in shooting all types of firearms.

Her beautiful but amoral mother, like her woman-chasing father, took no personal interest in her daughter, left her to be raised by a nanny. When her father was away on his many overseas business trips, her mother "entertained" masculine friends at their large estate southeast of Baltimore, down on Chesapeake Bay. Men from old moneyed families were continually bringing paramours to the estate, staying a few days and then leaving. Her mother had many lovers, men who had nothing better to do than bed-hop with bored wealthy spouses. It was a way of life for Maryland old-moneyed family dynasties. In their social circles, marriage fidelity was an unknown virtue.

The motivation to leave home came one spring day when

one of her mother's masculine friends, an older man she detested, raped her. It was then she realized the house in which she lived, while opulent with the appurtenances of wealth, was actually nothing more than a house of harlotry.

So she was sitting alone in a Baltimore tavern, nursing a late afternoon martini, wondering what to do, where to go to escape her unhappy existence. A tall handsome young attorney had been eyeing her from a corner booth. Recognizing her loneliness, State Senator Steven Hurst sauntered over, bought her a drink, flattered her with compliments. Within the hour he had her in his hotel suite, in bed. She found it to be an exciting night. Her pleasure came from teasing personal information from this young handsome attorney. Divorced and childless, he was dedicated to his political dream. He, too, was from an old blue-blood Maryland family whose fortune had been made generations earlier smuggling rum from Jamaica.

During that night of sexual passion he'd learned she was the sole heir to an old affluent Maryland family. Next morning he drove her thirty miles up-state to the family mansion inherited from his deceased parents. Here he gave her the dubious honor of being the second woman he'd permitted to live with him at the ancestral country estate.

After two months she discovered why his former wife had divorced him. One day when he was down in Baltimore, the family doctor phoned to inform him that medical science had discovered a new treatment for his illness, wanted him to come to the clinic to begin weekly injections. When she asked the doctor what his illness was, the doctor, thinking she was his wife, said, "Syphilis, I thought you knew." She was shocked!

Now, cowering in the large upstairs closet in the mansion's master bedroom, she finally heard him leave, heard him descending the marble stairway, heard him slam shut the front door, heard the distinctive roar of his Porsche as he drove away.

Within the closet she found a suitcase, quickly packed it, went to the steel safe hidden behind a bedroom wall painting, dialed the combination she'd secretly observed him refer to, numbers scribbled on the underside of the nightstand drawer. Inside were important documents she hastily threw onto the floor. Stashed in the rear were dozens of bundles of one hundred dollar bills, money from illegal payoffs received for his vote on certain legislative bills for favored lobbyists, money he didn't know she knew he had.

Later that evening she was on a train to Asheville, North Carolina, putting as much distance as she could between them. She was looking for a remote town where she could hide, a place where people would be different from everyone she'd known in her life, a place where no one would know her family, a place where she could begin a new life.

Two days later she was riding on a local Greyhound bus headed west to any destination beyond Asheville. The next day, in western North Carolina, she boarded a milk train whose ultimate destination was Atlanta, Georgia. After frequent stops at local mountain communities, the train finally crossed the north Georgia state line. A mechanical breakdown in the old locomotive forced it to lay over in Clermont, a town just south of the North Carolina border. The train conductor announced it would be at least three days before spare parts would arrive from Atlanta and repairs made. Passengers had to get off, walk two blocks up a hill to the local hotel where they could rent a room and wait until the rebuilt engine was able to continue its remaining ninety mile journey to Atlanta.

Peggy Trask, suitcase tightly gripped in her left hand, a suitcase that contained her few items of hastily packed clothing but, more importantly containing nearly $100,000 in cash. Weary from the uphill walk, she approached the main street Clermont Hotel with its stately white fluted columns outlining its broad wrap-around veranda. Breathing heavily, she ascended the six cement steps and onto the porch. There she paused, slowly turned to gaze up at the dogwood-covered mountains encircling the town. To herself she whispered, "This is the place. My destiny is here."

Chapter 3
Clermont, Georgia

Seated in a brown wicker rocking chair on the front veranda of the Clermont Hotel, Peggy Trask heard the beckoning whistle of the repaired locomotive as it called passengers to board for the six hour trip to Atlanta. She ignored its summons. In the past three days she'd received a better offer.

Waiting for the train crew to make engine repairs she'd become comfortable in this small north Georgia town. Her meals at the Clermont Café were good. The clean crisp mountain air was in sharp contrast to Baltimore's polluted industrial atmosphere. The warm sun and birth of spring had rejuvenated her previously depressed spirits. She was ready to live the remainder of her life in this quiet community.

That first evening in Clermont, seated in one of a dozen wicker chairs on the hotel veranda, Peggy and a dozen other marooned train passengers were watching the sun set over the western mountain range. She guessed that in this small mountain town watching colorful sunsets was the most exciting event of each day. Another delayed traveler, an attractive woman in her early 30's, a full glass of wine in hand, approached her.

"Hello. My name's Connie. Looks like you're also bored waiting in this hick town for our train to be repaired. Mind if I sit in this chair beside you and share the sunset?"

Glancing up, in a quick sweeping appraisal, Peggy noted she was wearing well tailored gabardine black slacks, a short sleeve pink satin blouse open at the neck, no makeup, and a bobbed hair style. "No. Please help yourself to the chair. However there's something about this quaint mountain town that appeals to me."

"You're obviously headed for Atlanta as I am." She eased herself down into the wicker chair, cautiously balancing her full glass of wine. She crossed her long legs, looked over at Peggy with a warm smile. "I noticed you when we first boarded the train in North Carolina.

"I also noticed you. We were the only two women on the train."

"For the past twelve years, I've lived in another hick town about eighty miles north of here, Johnson City, up in East Tennessee. My father's an attorney in Atlanta, with Coca Cola Corporation. He's promised me a position as a paralegal. Last week my divorce was finalized. I'd been married for twelve years. For eleven of those years my husband and I fought. Never had any children for which I'm thankful now that I'm single again."

"Sorry."

"How about you? You married? I don't see a ring on your finger. You look so young." She readjusted her position in the chair all the while keeping her eyes focused on Peggy as she took a sip of wine.

Peggy was mildly surprised by this stranger's spontaneous litany of personal information. Some strange previously untapped emotional compulsion within found this woman appealing. "Yes. I'm also headed for Atlanta. Not sure what I'll do there. If I don't like Atlanta I may move on to New Orleans. I've never been married, don't plan to be." As an afterthought, a point this woman's presence seemed to generate, she said, "Men turn me off." She flashed a mock smile at her new acquaintance.

As the two watched the sun's cusp slowly disappearing over the crest of the nearby mountain ridge, the evening sky became filled with evanescing reds, pinks and blue colors. Both silently observed this dazzling display. Darkness and cooler evening mountain air began invading the porch's veranda. Light from the hotel's main lobby was filtering out from its doors and windows, beckoning the sunset watchers to come inside. Tourists began wandering into the warmer lighted lobby to watch an old 1951 John Wayne movie, "Flying Leathernecks" on a black-and-white television screen mounted up on one wall. Others drifted into the barroom for a bedtime drink of their favorite alcoholic beverage. A few weary hotel guests ascended the circular stairway to their second floor room for an early night of sleep or whatever.

"It's getting cool out here. Won't you come up to my hotel room and share a bottle of French wine and compare reasons why we both hate men?"

"Okay. Why not? It's too early to go to bed." She followed Connie into the lobby and up the spiral stairway and into her new friend's room.

The dull evening of superficial conversation finally ended about nine. As Peggy was leaving, Connie unexpectedly stepped over and embraced her, kissing her on the cheek.

Startled by this sudden invasion of her body space, Peggy stepped back, gave Connie a curious look. Connie, with a slight slur in her speech, the result of the consumption of three-fourths of her own bottle of wine, said, "I hope my spontaneous display of affection didn't offend you. I've detected that we both have a deep inclination for genuine love, the kind of love men are incapable of giving us."

Facial muscles tensing, Peggy gave this woman a long inquisitive gaze. Unknown inner feelings had been stirred by another woman's embrace. She responded, "No. I'm not offended. I never realize two women could be attracted to one another… as I've been to you." After a moment's hesitation, she placed her hand on the door knob, twisted it, opened the door and backed out of the room as she said, "Goodnight."

Yet unaware of it, that evening changed the course of her life. Unfolding circumstances and a future close relationship to one of the communities leading citizens would further nourish this aberrant nature within her.

****

All tables and booths in the Clermont Café were occupied. A tall handsome gentleman asked, "May I share this table with you?" From his manner of asking she perceived that in this crowded restaurant sharing booth space was customary. "Yes," she responded, flashing him a stiff smile. "Be my guest."

As he sat down across from her he introduced himself. "My name's Charles Gist. May I have the pleasure of learning the identity of such a beautiful woman who's been so gracious as to allow me to share her table?"

Peggy hesitated, afraid her eastern accent would betray her as a stranger in this small southern town. She'd sensed "locals" were weary of strangers. But when her gaze met his, she somehow knew he didn't care. "My name's Peggy Trask. I'm one of those stranded passengers from the broken down train delayed here on its trip to Atlanta." Noting his approving smile, she added, "In Atlanta I've been promised employment as a secretary in the Veteran's Hospital." She was becoming good at lying. She had not the slightest prospect for work in Atlanta.

She guessed he must be at least ten years her senior.

Charles Gist had a possessive demeanor. He made her feel that in his presence nothing in this world could harm her. Flashing on the screen within her mind was an image of her father whom she hardly knew but always wanted to please. That likeness was immediately replaced by her recent nightmarish encounter with her Baltimore lover, the man who'd exposed her to a dreaded venereal disease, the man on whom she'd taken her revenge by stealing $100,000 of his secret slush fund, money he could never report as a theft because of its illegal origin. These brief thoughts made her body slightly shudder.

For a brief moment her eyes squeezed tightly together. She hoped he hadn't noticed her reflex. But, he had. He sensed vulnerability.

Gist had been a precocious student. At age seventeen he'd graduated from an elite private southern prep school. At age twenty he'd earned a bachelor's degree from Duke University. At age twenty-three he'd graduated from Duke's Law School. For the previous nine years he'd been an associate in a prestigious Atlanta law firm where his specialty was lawsuit litigation. A few miles north of Clermont his aged parents owned several thousand acres of rich valley farm land. Both his father and mother were in poor health. In the previous month Attorney Vaughn had resigned his position in Atlanta, moved to the mountains to set up his own law practice just to be near his parents, helping them manage rental arrangements on the dozen small tenant farms they owned and tightly controlled. The Gist's traced their ancestry back to the post-revolutionary era when a distant young grandfather's Caucasian wife in her early twenties died in childbirth. Her young widowed husband then married a hardy strong Cherokee woman whose back-breaking labor helped cut down trees, clear land, and build a cabin and raise six sons. Today, as an only child, the land holdings of his parents was land he'd someday inherit, rich bottom land, loamy black soil that produced bountiful crops. Like other "locals" owning land was very important to him.

Pretending to be reading the menu brought by the waitress

he was actually studying the woman across the table. Her youthful beauty enticed him. Next to owning land and having money, sex was important, more important than good food. Two years earlier he'd divorced his wife. His ex-wife had immediately remarried the senior partner in their Atlanta law firm. Prior to the divorce he himself had had several affairs with secretaries. After moving to Clermont he'd had a brief affair with a prominent divorced socialite in the nearby county seat town of Belton. It ended when she eloped with the local circuit judge.

As intelligent as he was, Charles Gist had no core moral values.

The demeanor of this attractive woman seated across the table told him she came from an affluent family. He'd noted her expensive clothing. The jacket lining briefly exposed when she returned the menus to the waitress displayed an exclusive French label. Her perfume said "expensive."

Peggy gave her order to the impatient waitress whose yellow and white uniform had pinned in the center of a pink lace hanky above her left breast a plastic name-tag that said "Maggie." Scribbling the order on a note pad, Maggie quickly headed for the kitchen.

Charles saw an opening "So you're going to Atlanta to become a secretary?"

"Yes." She made eye contact. He smiled in response.

"Do you know anything about legal contracts?"

"No." Her wandering eyes briefly focused on the wall above their booth, on a large black and white photo of Clermont's Main Street the way it was in the previous generation.

"Have you had any experience with lawsuits?"

"No." Her eyes averted his gaze. She was beginning to feel stressed with his interrogation.

He sensed her tension, wanted to reduce her uneasiness. "After breakfast, I'm driving out to one of the many small farms my parents own. I have to evict the tenants. They

16

haven't paid their rent for three months. They blame their non-payment on their old age and high medical bills."

"Does that trouble you, evicting two elderly people from their home?"

"No, not at all. It's not their house. They haven't paid their rent. They have to move out." Maggie placed a cup of coffee on the table before him. As he put a spoonful of sugar into the black coffee, he acknowledged her presence with a polite "Thank you." She returned his gratitude with a quick wink, a flirting smile and walked away.

Matter-of-factly, Peggy inquired, "Where will they go?"

"I don't know and don't care. That's their problem, not mine." He gave her a quick smile as the fingers of his right hand moved to his head and raked through unruly black hair strands. As he did so he said, "Business is business. There's no room for charity in business. I'm not a priest, not even religious. In fact I'm an atheist. If they don't pay the rent, they must move." He smiled, not at her, but at the thought of evicting two aged tenants.

For several long seconds she scrutinized him as he stirred his coffee. She found his calloused attitude about business intriguing, appealing. Through his view of life she was learning more about herself, who she really was.

"After we finish our meal, if you have time, I'd like to drive you around north Georgia and show you some of our beautiful lakes and waterfalls. Would you join me for such a morning tour, ending with a lunch at the quaint Bavarian Inn Restaurant down in Helen, Georgia, a German tourist town?"

"I'd like that. All I've seen of this region is scenery viewed through the sooty window of the train."

"Wonderful." As he spoke, in his mind a cunning thought was crystallizing. "Could I persuade you to stay here in Clermont and become my secretary?"

Startled at the spontaneous offer and weighing any

veiled intentions, she took a second more discerning look at him. She was drawn to his square proportioned head, his dimpled chin, muscular jaws and thick arched eyebrows which partially framed emerald green eyes. His head of black hair was already showing strands of gray. When he turned sideways to speak to the waitress she thought the profile of his face resembled the Indian head on a "buffalo nickel." Her attraction to his facial countenance morphed into thoughts about whether he was serious with this offer of employment? She glanced up to gaze into his face. He responded with a reflex motion of running the fingers of his right hand through the thick hair on his head, a gesture that was to become one of his identifying characteristics.

Their eyes made contact. At that precise moment Maggie returned to their booth, placed two steaming plates of food on the table before them. To give Peggy time to respond, he said, "Do you take cream and sugar in your coffee?" He was reaching to the end of the table for the sugar and cream dispensers.

"Yes, both." His attention to her needs in such a simple matter further attracted her to him. The lawyer in him perceived her elevated interest. As he lifted his cup of black coffee to his lips, he glanced into her face, especially into her eyes. He said, "I'm sorry to have been so blunt in my offer. In my law practice I'm beginning a class action lawsuit against an international insurance corporation. I need someone to do research on the huge number of potential plaintiffs. I suspect there may be as many as two thousand swindled individuals that would profit from a successful litigation against this mega corporation. Laying the legal foundation for a lawsuit will take several years to organize. I need someone to do all of this painstaking labor of compiling this list. If I'm successful my fee will be over five hundred million dollars. Take some time to think about it." A fleeting after thought reminded him that he didn't know if she could type, file, or take dictation.

She smiled. Their eyes again locked. Both knew what her answer would be.

Three days after arriving in Clermont, Peggy Trask ignored the beckoning whistle of the repaired departing train for Atlanta. She'd found her place to live. She'd become the full-time secretary for the newly formed Charles Gist Law Firm, and in time, perhaps more.

One week later, barrister Gist in a confidential conversation with his close friend, president of the town's only bank, learned that Peggy Trask had, one day after the repaired train departed Clermont, deposited ninety-five thousand dollars in cash in the local Bank. That information cinched his resolve.

One month after arriving in town, in a civil wedding in the Court House chambers of the Clermont County Probate Judge, Peggy Trask became the wife of Charles Gist. It was a corporate partnership more than a marriage, a legal contract for social respectability, a merger of selfish ambitions, a union of perverse beliefs, a consolidation of amoral spirits that in time would make them fabulously wealthy...but eternally damned.

CHAPTER 4
CLERMONT CAFÉ, 1959

As usual, the Clermont Café on downtown Main Street was crowded, serving breakfast to the town's business folk and the occasional tourist. The standard order: two eggs scrambled, country ham, wheat toast, coffee, and always grits. Full-time waitress, Maggie, and part-time waitresses Betty Ruth, and Audie, were busy catering to customers, many of whom had known one another from their school days. Five days a week, each morning and noon, this place was one big family dining room.

Wrapping around the outer edges of the floor are about twenty brown nagahyde-covered cushioned booths with green plastic-laminated table tops. The bottom five feet of the surrounding walls are lined with dark oak wainscot panels. The upper walls are textured plaster painted an aqua color, paint which is beginning to chip near the ceiling. In the center floor section are about three dozen yellow Formica-topped tables with attached bench seats that flip up and down. All booths and tables seat up to four people, except one large circular corner booth that seats as many as eight.

On the side walls, spaced at eye level, are dozens of large black-framed yellowish photographs of the way the town looked about two generations earlier. Prominent is a photograph of the old hotel before it was destroyed by fire in the late fall of 1948. Most folk have seen the vacant land where it was once located just north of the cobblestone Methodist Church building at the south end of Main Street. The only remaining part is the wide solid concrete steps that once led up from the sidewalk to its grand veranda. The photograph clearly shows these steps, steps now leading to nowhere, a ghostly reminder that Clermont was not what it once had been. Change in Clermont is caused only by calamity. The passing years are identified by these periodic destructive events.

Another photo catches the eye, a 1930's scene on Main Street. It's Smith's Texaco Gas Station with its white brick columns supporting a red-tiled canopy under which stood two gas pumps. A sign advertises gasoline for eighteen point nine cents a gallon. In that photo another feature catches the viewer's attention. It's Sam Smith, the original owner, with both hands on the handle of the pump which had to be pushed back-and-forth to lift volatile fluids up into a tall clear-glass cylinder marked off at regular intervals with numbers identifying gallons. Gravity caused gasoline to flow into thirsty auto gas tanks below. "Locals" now know the old redecorated gas station as the "Bill Stoddard Insurance Agency." In one corner of its office area are dozens of wooden racks holding thousands of antique post cards, a most unusual commodity, items Bill's wife sells to tourist collectors.

Among the dozen other wall photos is one showing the town drug store located across the street from the cafe. Many "locals" remember buying ice cream sodas at its counter, then sitting on heavy steel wire chairs pulled up to small opaque glass-top tables with black metal rims. The ice cream counter, chairs and tables, are still there and used.

The most prominent photograph, the one that catches the attention of tourists who wander into the cafe is near the front door, directly behind the cash register. It's a glossy back-and-white print of the then "King of Hollywood" Clark Gable, star of the 1938 movie, *"Gone with the Wind,"* eating lunch at the Clermont Café. It was taken in 1947 when he was on tour promoting his latest movie *"The Hucksters."* Retired as a WW II Major from the 8th Army Air Force, he'd earned the Distinguished Flying Cross for bravery under enemy fire. As a zealous life-long Republican and knowing he was in the very heart of the Democratic Party in Dixie, beside his name he'd teasingly scribbled *"God bless Georgia Republicans."* Even Democrats are amused when reading his comment. His past visit to the Clermont Cafe gives credence to the tourist's judgment this is a good place to eat. It also has a subliminal message that Clermont is not some little mountain hick town.

In the rear section of the restaurant is a large solid oak table, an unchanged historic relic for fond memories of the "locals." People often comment, "If that table could only talk, the stories it could tell." This unobtrusive platform for gustatory delights is the one item in this eating emporium that has remained constant since the café first opened its doors in 1920. Lined up on each side of this imposing walnut antique are ten sturdy chairs, their seats shiny as a testimony to the thousands of cloth bottoms that have slid across their surfaces. In the middle of the table top is a brown-yellow tent-fold piece of thick plastic on which are engraved on both sides two words, "LIAR'S TABLE."

As usual, each chair surrounding the "Liar's Table" is occupied with a local man. Outsiders and women never would dare sit at this table. Each man who eats here is a prominent high-ranking Clermont citizen: the bank president, the postmaster, the editor of the weekly County newspaper, the school superintendent, the developer of the new resort just outside town, the county sheriff, county commissioners, the mayor and/or city councilmen, and of course the County's leading physician, Dr. Henry Paige. One man comes, eats, talks and then leaves. Immediately another dignitary enters the café, sits down in his empty chair. These men have kept the same breakfast and lunch schedule for years. Like clockwork, each knows precisely when to arrive, when to leave.

Around this table more business deals have been finalized than at the nearby court house. Conversations often lead to some agreement, followed by a grunt of approval or disapproval. Not even a handshake is necessary. These men are the community movers and shakers. In each of their minds the rigid social power structure is clearly defined. Each knows the exact limits of the other's turf. No outsider would ever dare intrude into this county pecking order, a political hierarchy that dates back to pioneer days in the early nineteen hundreds. These men will frequently disagree about college football teams, major league baseball teams, who the prettiest girl in town is or was, but, they never disagree about the limits of the power each possesses. All are land owners... and "financially comfortable."

Inside the Clermont Café on this April Monday morning, as usual, every booth was filled. The conversation chatter was loud. If one wanted to eaves drop on folk in the next booth just inches away, it would have been difficult. But, no one really wants to listen to gossip in the next booth. In this small town, there are seldom any new secrets.

It was about seven-fifteen in the morning when a tall young man with the build of a basketball player, lean but stocky, a man probably in his middle twenties, pushed open the thick glass aluminum framed door, stood there for a few moments as his eyes adjusted to the dimmer light inside. Patrons who looked up saw him silhouetted in the door opening like John Wayne entering a western saloon in an old 1940 Hollywood movie. For a few seconds all conversation ceased as most glanced at this impressive stranger. He had a confident demeanor that seemed bold, perhaps even aggressive, yet controlled. His eyes scanned the customers, seemingly looking for one particular person. His eyes quickly fixed on a middle aged man in a white smock coat seated at the Liar's Table. As the glass door behind him slowly swung shut, he made his way through crowded tables, side-stepping three busy waitresses as he maintained his visual fix on his targeted man seated at the long table in the rear of the restaurant.

He stopped behind the man with the short cropped salt-pepper beard, the man wearing a white coat, obviously a physician because he had the symbol of his profession, a shinny stethoscope, hanging limply around his neck. Conversation around the table continued, each man aware of the stranger's presence, but choosing to ignore him. Finally the young man politely tapped the shoulder of the bearded physician. "Excuse me, sir," he said. "Are you Doctor Paige?"

The older man turned, looked up at this six foot five inch man standing behind him and slightly to his left, responded, "Yes. What business is it to you who I am?"

"I'm Doctor Gustav Ginther. Forgive me for interrupting you while you're eating breakfast. I'm in my second year of psychiatry residency down at Emory. I'll finish in about six months. I'm exploring possibilities of where I might set up a future practice. I've always loved these mountains, used to vacation here as a youngster. I thought I might settle here and practice both medicine and psychiatry. I was over at Memorial Hospital and there asked the administrator if I could tour the facilities."

Page interrupted, "Our hospital administrator doesn't have time to give tours at my hospital."

Gus gave the older doctor a broad smile as he was being visually psychoanalyzed by the steely eyes of the older practitioner of the medical art. Feeling ill-at-ease and out-of-place, Ginther said, "That's what the administrator told me. He said to come to you as the chief-of-staff. Is it possible for you to give me permission to inspect the facilities? I'm under pressure to be back in Atlanta at three this afternoon."

Ginther had that same feeling when many years ago, as a first grader, he'd once raised his hand to seek his teacher's permission to go to the school toilet.

Scowling, Paige's eyes continued scanning this young man who had intruded into his breakfast conversation. He snarled, "We got enough doctors already in this County. We don't need another one, especially a psychiatrist. Go back to Atlanta. Set up your practice there. Everyone living in Clermont County is sane and doesn't need a shrink. Establish your practice somewhere else." He turned, readjusted his chair and resumed his conversation with the man seated next to him.

"As I said before that young jackass interrupted me, you're in the road paving business. I need to have the driveway up to my house blacktopped. Can we work out a swap? Free hospital and medical service for you and your family for twelve months in exchange for 300 feet of asphalt?"

Ginther stood silent, feeling the sting of Paige's rebuke. He slowly turned, walked back to the front door, his emotions obviously injured. As he stepped out of the door and into the invigorating fresh morning mountain air, he stood motionless, wondering what to do next. He could return to the local hospital and try to bluff his way into getting a tour of the facilities, or he could begin on his return two hour trip to Atlanta, forget Clermont and his dream of someday practicing his skills here. His gaze wandered upward, caught a brief glimpse of the restaurant's art deco sign over his head, and then focused on the large rock out-cropping on the distant mountain the locals called, "Sugar Loaf Mountain," a landmark that loomed high above the valley in which the city of Clermont nestled.

For several seconds he starred at this promontory, then heard himself muttering, "That damned doctor's afraid I'm going to take away some of his practice. There's room in this growing region for both of us. I'll teach him I'm not easily dissuaded. This community needs a good physician." He paused, then added, "...and a good psychiatrist. My future is here."

CHAPTER 5
MEMORIAL HOSPITAL,
CIRCA 1960

"Hello." The voice on the other end of the telephone line sounded sleepy. It was, four thirty Saturday morning.

"Doctor Queen?"

"Yeah?"

"This is Janice over in ER. A Margaret Goodwin has just come in complaining of a severe sore throat. Doctor Rolf checked her, determined she has strep throat, gave her ten milligrams morphine to ease her pain. Rolf wanted you informed, since she's your patient. He's waiting for your further orders. Do you remember her?"

"Yeah." He paused, then continued, his sleepy voice quiet, "I see her about something-or-other in my office every month. I know her tolerance level. Admit her. Give her the regular dosage of penicillin. Then give her ten more milligrams of morphine I.M. Q.I.D. when she gets settled in her room. I'll see her mid morning."

"That's it? You don't want to come in, examine her for yourself? Are you concerned about respiratory failure, concerned about her being allergic to penicillin?"

"No. If Rolf diagnosed her with strep throat and ordered penicillin, that's good enough for me. I just returned from my grandson's birthday party in Greenville. I'm too tired to come over. I'll see her later today. Goodnight."

At Memorial Hospital Janice scribbled Queen's orders on Mrs. Goodwin's chart, then on a note pad beside the phone, walked over to where Rolf was waiting beside the gurney where his patient was struggling for each breath of air.

"Here," she said matter-of-factly as she handed Queen's orders to Rolf. He took the slip of paper, stuck it in his coat pocket and began the routine of admitting Mrs. Goodwin. Within a few minutes a sleepy orderly appeared, wheeled Mrs. Goodwin out of ER to an elevator, while Doctor Rolf went to the family waiting room to talk to Mr. Goodwin.

"Nothing serious," he said to the anxious husband whose twelve-year old son and ten-year-old daughter were sleeping in chrome-cushioned chairs. "Doctor Queen ordered medicine to relieve her pain and a dose of penicillin. He wants to keep her here twenty-four hours for observation. He'll be in to check her later today, probably about noon. I suggest you all go home. Phone the hospital later this evening to check on her condition. Most likely your wife will be discharged tomorrow."

"Thanks doc. My mind's relieved. This all came on her so fast. When we left Atlanta about midnight she wasn't feeling good. An hour later, she could hardly swallow."

"The medicine should help her sleep. In about eight hours the swelling in her throat should be down. Go home. Get some sleep. Your wife will be in room 226 if you want to visit her this evening."

Up on the second floor night nurse Godfrey, at her station desk, was looking at Mrs. Goodwin's chart, noted medication ordered by Doctor Queen. She went to the narcotics cabinet, unlocked it, took out a vial of morphine, picked up a sterile syringe package, locked the cabinet, headed for room 226. She found Mrs. Goodwin gulping for each breath, her inflamed throat slowly constricting. Efficiently Nurse Godfrey injected the narcotic, withdrew the needle, threw the syringe in the special waste container near the bed. At that precise moment, her beeper sounded. She hastened out of the room to the nurse's station, picked up the phone, said, "Second floor, Godfrey speaking. What's up?"

"All hell's broken loose here in ER. Bad car wreck out on the expressway. One code six, two more code four's. Another ambulance radioed it's on the way with two more victims. We're short staffed. Come help us until we can get some local on-call doctors out of bed and over here."

"I'm on my way."

****

Two hours later it was time for the Saturday hospital shift to check in. Nurse Godfrey, now back up on the second floor, was swamped with demands from the highway accident victims. At 7:30 her replacement, day Nurse Whalen, arrived. She immediately consulted with Godfrey who told her, "You take care of our regulars. I'll work overtime 'til these auto causalities are stabilized." She promptly disappeared down the hall.

Nurse Whalen walked over to the patient chart rack, found the new chart for Mrs. Goodwin, lifted it out, scrutinized it, noted Rolf's injection of ten milligram's morphine in ER, saw Doctor Queen's orders for another dosage of ten milligrams morphine, saw there was no record it had been given, went to the narcotic cabinet, unlocked it, took out a vial, picked up an injection package, headed for room 226. She found Mrs. Goodwin in a deep sleep. The experienced nurse deftly extracted the sterile needle from the hypodermic package, filled it with the prescribed dosage, injected Mrs. Goodwin as ordered by Doctor Queen. As she rubbed Mrs. Goodwin's buttock where the needle had pierced the skin, she observed

Mrs. Goodwin's body begin to twitch, then convulsions, showed signs of respiratory depression, cardiac arrest. Instinctively she reached for Mrs. Goodwin's wrist, found her pulse, was shocked to feel it so strong, like it was ready to rupture the skin. Suddenly, no pulse! Mrs. Goodwin's body became comatose, motionless, lifeless.

Whalen punched the room emergency button. A doorbell-like chime began repeatedly pinging throughout hospital halls, a sound not offensive to visitor and patients, but an urgent alarm to all the medical staff. Within one minute, an orderly wheeled into room 226 a cart containing emergency cardiac arrest equipment. Rolf rushed in, began following emergency procedures for heart failure. The room was now filled with two more nurses, a local doctor who'd just entered the hospital for surgery scheduled for eight a.m.

At seven forty-nine the fight to save the life of Mrs. Goodwin was over. They'd lost the battle. She was dead. Their valiant efforts failed to revive her.

Nurse Whalen immediately phoned Doctor Queen at his home. Since he lived less than two miles from the hospital, he promised to be there in minutes.

Hospital administrator, Bill Mulligan, arrived in his office at his usual time, 7:30. As he was sorting through the night's admissions he heard the emergency alarm, noted it came from room 226, rushed up, entered the room, quickly analyzed the situation. He ordered everyone out of the room except for Doctor Rolf, nurses Godfrey and Whalen. Nurse Whalen told him she'd already called Doctor Queen and he'd arrive within minutes. Mulligan picked up Mrs. Goodwin's chart from the patient's bedside table where nurse Whalen had hurriedly placed it. Flipping through the few pages, he saw Doctor Queen's four thirty a.m. order for morphine. He quickly noted the chart contained no signature that the dosage had been administrated by night nurse Godfrey. Turning to

Godfrey, he asked, "No signature here? Did you give her the prescribed dosage of morphine? What time?"

Nurse Godfrey leaned over to look at the nearly blank page. She gasped, put her hand over her mouth, slumped into the chair in the corner of the room.

Bill Mulligan turned to nurse Whalen. She knew the question he was about to ask. "You saw Doctor Queen's order? Did you give Mrs. Goodwin the dosage he ordered?"

"Oh my God!" replied Nurse Whalen. She reached over, took hold of the hand of Nurse Godfrey. "We BOTH gave her the dosage!"

Before retiring for the first time, Bill Mulligan had been a career administrator at a U.S. Naval hospital in Tampa, Florida. He was in his second career at this small mountain hospital. He knew exactly what to do. He had to save the career of these two dedicated loyal nurses, save the career of Doctor Queen, and most importantly, save the reputation of his hospital. He turned and said, "Under no circumstances are you to admit anyone else to this patient's room. I'm going to my office. I'll be back within minutes." He dashed out of the room.

In his office he pickup his private telephone line, dialed Doctor Paige's office phone number. Paige's office was just across the street from the hospital. He knew Paige always came to his office early Saturday morning to plan his schedule for the coming week. Then at 9:30 he'd leave to walk the short block to his church where the choir rehearsed hymns for the worship service the next day, Sunday. Paige had a strong tenor voice.

"Henry?"

"Yes."

"This is Mulligan over in my office. I suggest you get over here PDQ. If you're not here in minutes, this place will explode. We have a dire emergency. I can't keep the lid on for more than fifteen minutes. Come to room 226. Talk to no one on your way here."

"I'll be there in seconds." Click.

In room 226 Doctor Rolf and the two nurses continued to administer emergency treatment to the dead Mrs. Goodwin, though it was obvious their efforts were for naught. Within minutes Paige appeared, walked over to the bed, instinctively felt for the pulse of Mrs. Goodwin. None. Bill Mulligan concisely explained the situation. He knew that his hospital, Doctor Queen and nurse Godfrey all faced malpractice lawsuits if word of this error leaked out. Nurse Godfrey acknowledged her mistake of not making an entry in the patient's chart for the 4:30 a.m. dosage. Nurse Whalen was judged innocent, but was deeply disturbed that it was her injection that had actually caused the patient's death.

At eight ten a.m. Doctor Queen arrived in room 226. Instinctively he too checked Mrs. Goodwin for vital signs. None. For several seconds Paige now in charge, paced back and forth around the bed, re-checking the dead woman's pulse, placing his stethoscope to listen for the faintest of heart beats. Turning to Rolf he ordered him to fetch an all-purpose emergency cart. A minute or two later, after the cart arrived, he lifted the sheet from the dead woman's body and deftly made an incision in Mrs. Goodwin's groin. The plan was to use saline solution to flush out any morphine residue in her blood vessels. Later they'd explain to coroner Bill Hamilton that in the hospital they'd already started to prepare her body for embalming.

Hamilton owned the only funeral home in Clermont County. As a "local" it was natural he'd be elected as county coroner, a political position he'd held for the previous twenty years. He was a first cousin to Bill Mulligan's wife. In the past he'd helped cover up other hospital errors, none as serious as this. He could be trusted to keep quiet.

The administrator of Memorial Hospital and the local

sheriff frequently sent out-of-area accident fatalities to George Hamilton's funeral home where the price for embalming was three times the rate charged locals. Each Christmas George Hamilton sent the sheriff and Bill Mulligan an expensive gift of some kind or another. The sheriff, Howard Lammars, Memorial hospital chief of staff, Doctor Paige, the hospital administrator, Bill Mulligan, and the Hamilton Funeral Home had a sweet cozy relationship with one another.

So Paige, assisted by Rolf and Doctor Queen, flushed out the evidence of morphine overdose, altered Mrs. Goodwin's chart to read that Doctor Queen's order for ten milligrams of morphine had in fact been properly administered at 4:30 a.m. by nurse Godfrey, after Rolf had given her ten milligrams in ER. All agreed to the story that when nurse Whalen checked room 226 at 7:30 a.m. Mrs. Goodwin was experiencing respiratory failure and a major heart attack caused by an allergic reaction to the penicillin.

The death of Mrs. Goodwin was a tragic unforeseen accident that might have happened in the best big city hospitals. Fatal allergic reactions to antibiotics, while not common, did happen.

At twelve noon Bill Mulligan mournfully notified Ed Goodwin that his wife had unexpectedly died of a massive heart attack. Her body was taken to the Hamilton Funeral Home for final embalming. Viewing by friends and family at Hamilton Funeral Home was on Tuesday evening. The funeral was Wednesday at 1 p.m. at First Methodist Church. Included in the crowd of mourners for this mother of two young children and her widower husband were Doctor Queen, Nurse Whalen, Nurse Godfrey, hospital administrator Bill Mulligan, and Doctor Paige. Ed Goodwin received comfort from the fact that the entire Memorial Hospital medical staff had taken time from their busy schedule to attend his wife's funeral.

A month after Mrs. Goodwin's death, within the

community word leaked out from some unknown source that Ed Goodwin had hired Attorney Charles Gist who had filed a three million dollar lawsuit against the hospital, against its liability insurance carrier, against Doctor Paige, Bill Mulligan, Doctor Queen, Nurses Whalen and Godfrey, against each of the three County Commissioners who had oversight of Memorial Hospital. Both Attorney Gist and Atlanta attorneys for the insurance carrier immediately subpoenaed all hospital records.

Attorney Gist filed charges of criminal negligence against Nurse Whalen who had administered the fatal drug. Before the grand jury this ploy caused Nurse Whalen to break down emotionally and give an exact detailed account of what happened the morning Mrs. Goodwin died. Her testimony incriminated Doctor Paige as the instigator of the cover-up.

The grand jury's indictment of Doctor Paige and Memorial Hospital proved to the attorney's for the defendant insurance company they had no case. Except for Paige and the hospital itself, charges against all others listed in the lawsuit were dropped. An out-of-court settlement was the best hope for the insurance company to minimize their losses. Attorney Gist advised Ed Goodwin that the dollar amount in his lawsuit should be reduced to one million dollars, thus avoiding a drawn-out expensive jury trial.

Since Doctor Paige, as Chief-of-Staff, had orchestrated the medical negligence cover-up, the insurance company for the hospital threatened to sue him if he didn't pay half of the compensation settlement. The Circuit Judge ordered Paige to personally pay five hundred thousand dollars. Since Paige's vanity had kept him from ever buying expensive medical malpractice insurance, paying this amount brought him to the edge of bankruptcy. The Judge ordered the insurance carrier for the hospital to pay to the defendant an amount equal to Paige's. Thus Ed Goodwin received one million dollars for compensation for the wrongful death of his beloved wife and mother of his two children.

Part of the final out-of-court agreement demanded by Paige was that the hospital be given a clean report on all charges against it, and that both parties in the litigation must not reveal the terms of the private out-of-court settlement.

Doctor Paige was forced to mortgage his house and drain his savings in order to pay his penalty of five hundred thousand dollars. Bill Mulligan's penalty for his role in the cover up was $50,000 but was covered by his liability insurance.

Attorney Gist's fee for his services was just over two hundred thousand dollars.

Although gossip in Clermont was rampant, folk in the community were never publicly informed of any malfeasance in their health care system, the core of which was Memorial Hospital, the one institution to which all "locals" had at one time or another formed a strong bond. Many of their babies had been born in this building. Many aged parents had taken their last breath here. Others had been a patient when bones were broken, or tonsils or an appendix removed. Community pride ran deep for this hallowed structure and for its long time Chief-of-Staff, Doctor Henry Paige.

Nurse Whalen died of brain cancer six months after the settlement. Three years later Nurse Godfrey was well on her way to becoming an alcoholic.

Doctor Queen moved his office into the building across the street from the hospital, a medical facility owned by Doctor Paige. He paid double the rent he'd paid for his old location in the second floor of the downtown bank building. His public rationale for moving was that the new office was "closer to the hospital."

Outwardly Paige remained the beloved bearded country physician, but inwardly he was seething with hate for Attorney Gist.

Six months after the confidential settlement, the *Clermont*

Clarion printed several of the charges of incompetence Gist had made against Paige. Paige threatened to sue both the newspaper and Gist for violating confidential terms of the court settlement. The community rallied to support Doctor Paige. The newspaper editor printed an apology. An editorial on page four stated that their information was incorrect. The editor then began a four week series about Paige's competence in past medical crises, stories to certify him as the County's beloved physician.

Three years after his wife's death, Ed Goodwin remarried. Everyone in the community said his new wife was a good woman and deserved high praise for taking on the chore of raising Ed's two teenage children. Ed moved his family to rural South Georgia where he purchased a 200 acre cotton farm complete with large house, barns, and farm machinery, all for 800,000 dollars. Life in Clermont returned to normal. The town's hospital continued to be the most sacred institution in Clermont County.

Doctor Paige and Attorney Gist never visited the Clermont Café for breakfast at the same time. Paige ate at exactly 7a.m.. Gist at precisely 9:30 a.m.

Paige and Gist became bitter enemies. Paige privately vowed to even the score someday. Everyone in Clermont County knew the smoldering enmity between them would surely resurface. Because of their vanity and lack of integrity, neither could ever forgive the other. Attorney Gist had won only the first round in this feud. The power structure in Clermont waited for the second round.

CHAPTER 6
PEGGY GIST'S VISIT TO
DR. PAIGE, SUMMER 1966

"Doctor Paige's office, Gretchen speaking."

"Hello Gretchen. This is Peggy Gist. How are you today?"

"Fine, Peggy. You okay?" Gretchen had an annoying speech pattern. Nearly every sentence she uttered was followed by an overuse of the word 'okay', usually as a question. "Congratulations to you and your husband. Okay? I just read in this week's newspaper about Charles winning that class action lawsuit against Herrod's Supermarkets. Okay! I guess you and Charlie will be taking a trip to Hawaii with your share of the million dollar settlement."

"That's what I wanted to do for our next wedding anniversary. I've never been to Hawaii. However Charles has other plans, like investing in some business he's heard about from his buddies down in Atlanta. But he promised to take me to Asheville where we'll stay five days at the Grove Park Inn."

"Okay! That's the most exclusive lodge in the South. You'll be able to get all kinds of personal attention there, like body rubs, mud baths and facials. You'll come back to us looking like a Hollywood movie star." Lest Peggy think Gretchen was implying she was not already beautiful Gretchen quickly added, "Did you want to make an appointment with Doctor Paige?"

Peggy hesitated before answering. Many thoughts were racing through her mind. Making this appointment with Doctor Paige was risking her husband's wrath if he discovered she'd gone to Paige for consultation. In this small community, however, there wasn't much of a choice for doctors. Doctor Queen was always pushing "holistic herbal medicines" on his patients. Doctor Rolf had a reputation of being "knife happy," often prescribing surgery when it wasn't needed. The other three doctors in the community had questionable medical pedigrees, having graduated from medical schools down in the Caribbean.

"Peggy?" Gretchen said. "Are you there? Are you okay?"

With her voice lowered Peggy answered, "Gretchen, I need to make an appointment with the good doctor yet today, if at all possible. I've not been feeling at my best for the past few weeks. Then yesterday Charles flew out of Atlanta with six of his hunting friends for dove shooting down in Argentina. He won't return for two weeks. Last night I received a telegram that my parents who lived in Baltimore, parents I haven't seen in years, were killed in a small commuter airplane crash in south France. Tomorrow I'll be catching a flight to Paris to bring their bodies back to America. I need to have Dr. Paige prescribe a sedative to help me make that long sad trip. Will you make an appointment for me today, this morning, if possible?"

"Certainly Peggy. Please accept my sympathy on the death of your parents. How about four-thirty this afternoon? You'll be his last patient for the day. Okay?"

"That's fine. May I use the back door and go directly to the exam room, avoiding the waiting room?"

"Okay. I'll do that. You can park directly behind the clinic, ring the bell by the door. I'll usher you directly to an examination room. No one will ever know you're here. Okay?"

"Thanks Gretchen. I know I can trust you not to say anything about my visit. I prefer to keep the death of my parents out of our local newspaper. Neither of my parents were the best parents, and I don't want to spend the next few weeks being a hypocrite about their death."

"I understand. Your confidence will be safe with me."

Gretchen placed the phone back in its cradle, muttering to herself, "I wonder why that bitch wants to see the doctor. There's more to her request for an appointment than she told me. I can read her chart later after Paige sends it down to my desk."

****

At 4:35 Doctor Paige came into small exam room number three, saw Peggy Gist seated on the hard oak chair. He gave her a smile as he mentally noted the expensive tailored suit, shoes, expensive jewelry she was wearing. He put out his hand, touched her lightly on the shoulder. "Hi Peggy. Gretchen didn't write on the preliminary exam sheet why you wanted to see me. It just says, 'Personal.'" He gave her a clinical look, noting the many lines in her facial skin, lines known medically as, "smoker's face."

"Are you still smoking two packs a day, Peggy?"

"Doctor, mind your own business." Peggy flashed him a half smile as a hint to keep such questions to himself and at the same time letting him know she was friendly.

"Sorry." His cold apology lacked sincerity. There was a brief impasse in the conversation. He liked putting this woman on the defensive. It gave him an advantage in dealing with her. Hating her husband for suing him was a bitter memory. He sensed that because she'd come to him with

39

a health problem this might be an opportunity, somehow, for wreaking revenge upon her husband. She could afford to have gotten an appointment with an expensive Atlanta physician.

His criticism of her tobacco habit irritated her. "No doctor, I'm down to just one pack a day," she snobbishly replied. "I cough my lungs out for the first hour after I get out of bed each morning and..." glancing up toward the ceiling, "...I know I smoke too much, but that's not why I'm here." She lowered her voice as she saw a shadow appear below the half-inch space at the bottom of the closed door. She suspected Gretchen was eavesdropping outside the door. She also suspected that Gretchen and the good country doctor were more than employee and employer.

"For the past three months I've been having a vaginal discharge accompanied by soreness and a red inflamed opening to my vagina. Charles won't have anything to do with me, has taken to sleeping in a separate bedroom. I'm beginning to get suspicious about his weekly trips to Atlanta. He says he goes to visit his buddies for a day of golf, but I don't believe him. As if having marital problems wasn't enough, now I have this physical problem."

Her revelation of a marital problem heightened Paige's sense of interest.

She reached for a tissue on the nearby counter, brushed the corner of her eyes to remove tears forming, lightly touching herself so as not to smudge her mascara. "To make matters worse, yesterday I received a telegram that both my parents have been killed in an airplane accident while traveling in France. Tomorrow I leave Atlanta for Paris to return their bodies to the States and a quick burial in Baltimore. With this physical problem there's no way I can travel." Tear drops again appeared in her eyes. "My doctor in Atlanta couldn't work me into his schedule for another week." Tears were now slowly rolling down her cheeks.

His emotions not effected by her tears, Paige reacted. "There's not much I can do about problems two and three. Let's see what we can do about this vaginal discharge. I'll have Gretchen come and drape you, prepare for a pelvic exam. I can take some swab samples, send them to the Atlanta lab. By the time you return from Paris we'll know what the problem is." He paused and then added, "Until we get back the lab report, I'll give you some ointment that will allow you to travel without discomfort."

"Does Gretchen have to come in here? Can't you drape me for the exam? This is a very personal matter with me."

The brow of his forehead furled as he gave her a questioning look. "That personal, uh?" He stepped over to the linen closet, from the shelf took a green cotton drape as he said, "I'll step out of the room for a few minutes while you remove your panties and skirt and put on this gown. Then get up on the table, lay on your back. Okay?"

As he was inserting chrome leg stirrups into the table sockets he now knew this could be his long awaited opportunity to have his revenge on her husband for suing him, taking from him nearly a half million dollars, nearly sending him into bankruptcy.

****

TWO WEEKS LATER

"Hello Peggy. This is Gretchen at Doctor Paige's office, okay? Doctor Paige told me about the death of your parents. I know you've just returned from Paris and from the funeral for your parents. You must be emotionally drained but Doctor Paige wants to see you in his office this afternoon at three, okay? While you were in France your report came back from the Atlanta lab. Can you be here at three this afternoon?"

"Is there some serious problem, Gretchen? Have you seen the report?"

"No. These reports go directly to Doctor Paige for his eyes only, okay?" Gretchen was lying. "He just asked me to set up the appointment."

"Thanks Gretchen. I'll be there at three. Will you admit me again through the back door as before?"

"Okay."

****

"Hello Peggy. Please take a seat." Paige directed her to a maroon leather seat in front of his cluttered office desk.

As she took a seat Paige walked around the desk and took his seat. He picked up a blue file folder, opened it, quickly scanned the sheet, then looking up, making eye contact with his patient, a serious expression on his face, he spoke. "In my practice in this rural community I don't see many reports like this, for which I'm glad." He put down the folder, removed his eye glasses, sat back in his swivel chair, raised his head, with his right hand stroked his beard, and for a brief moment gazed up at the ceiling, and then sighed.

"What? What?" she asked, her face drawn, eyes intent on his expression.

"Before I tell you the results of the swab tests, I want you to know there's a treatment for what you have. This diagnosis is far from hopeless." He paused.

Peggy shifted her body to the edge of the chair, took a deep breath, held it for several seconds before she said, "What?"

"You are in the early secondary stage of syphilis."

Peggy Gist slumped over in the chair and fainted.

CHAPTER 7
TOM OWENS BUILDS HIS ADDICTION CLINIC, CIRCA 1968-1969

The entire Clermont community was buzzing with the news that the son of Reverend Owens was returning to the area and establishing an addiction clinic on forty acres secretly purchased on the western edge of the city. In the previous twenty-eight years, since 1940, his parents had been missionaries in the Philippines. In that interval their son Tom had not only become a physician but also had developed a deep concern for curing those addicted to illegal drugs. For him to reappear out of nowhere and chose their remote mountain region to establish a clinic for addicts raised many questions in the minds of Clermont County citizens.

Where did he obtain the financing for such a large project? Why an addiction rehabilitation center? Would Clermont now be over-run with drug addicts? Would people in Clermont now experience a high crime rate such as existed in Atlanta? Why did he choose to create such a clinic in this remote part of the nation? What effect would this healing center have on the existing Memorial Hospital, an institution sacred to people in northern Georgia? Why didn't he first approach Clermont government officials and seek their blessing for such a large project? Had he gone through proper government channels to be licensed to establish a hospital for drug dependent people?

Dr. Paige thought he knew the answers to the many questions being raised. Seated at his table in the Clermont Café he did not hesitate to tell everyone the money for such an expensive project was being supplied by drug cartels in South America. Why not? His logic seemed plausible. With their lucrative multimillion dollar profits from selling cocaine and marijuana in the U.S.A. they had caused the American government to create a multimillion dollar police force to counteract drug smuggling and concomitant crime that followed. The government program, known euphemistically as "The War on Drugs," was politically profitable. Thousands of men and women had become part of the bureaucracy created to fight this battle. What better course for the South American drug cartel to follow than to covertly establish their own program to cure those addicted to their profitable product? Making cocaine usage respectable would exponentially multiply their sales.

He was quick to point out that the liquor industry had once been illegal but now was a legitimate part of American culture. Just as state lotteries were once considered illegal as well as sinful, gambling casinos were now fashionable. Just as prostitution once considered immoral, now Nevada brothels were legal and a source of taxes, a tax source other states were considering. The billion dollar illegal drug business was now moving toward respectability and the even greater profits that respectability would bring.

That was Paige's explanation for South American funding of Tom Owens' four million dollar addiction clinic. Many who heard him expound his theory were convinced of its soundness.

Medical experts in both Europe and America were teaching that addiction to drugs was a disease, a disease that could be cured. American pharmaceutical companies were reaping huge profits with newly created legal drugs to "cure" those addicted to illegal drugs. Doctor Tom Owens was viewed by many as a visionary, a leader in the birth of a nationwide program for individuals seeking to overcome dependency on alcohol, cocaine, amphetamines and even marijuana.

Thus Doctor Paige successfully poisoned the minds of many in the Clermont community about the new Owens' medical center. And to fuel his contention, he always pointed out that Tom Owens, the invisible backer, was never present in the community to oversee his projected clinic and answer questions. Where was he? What did he have to hide? What did he look like? Was he a phantom or did he really exist?

Others, however, were elated that in their remote region such a program was being launched. Area business men saw the creation of a national drug rehabilitation center as the answer to the current economic slump. They envisioned high ranking government officials visiting Clermont to give publicity to the Owens' human reclamation project, envisioned glamorous Hollywood movie stars coming for cures for their drug addictions.

Local builders were being hired for construction of the elaborate medical complex on the fringe of their city. Since the local railroad had gone bankrupt back in the late 1950's major access to the community was only by a two lane Federal highway. Down in the Atlanta State Capital, under the Golden Dome State House, the North Georgia Democratic Representative and the District Republican State Senator were cooperating to fund the Department of Transportation so they could extend a four lane highway into

Clermont, an expressway that had terminated about thirty miles south of the Clermont County line. To support the anticipated arrival of many world-wide dignitaries, County Commissioners created a search committee to find enough flat land for a regional County airport, a sky port to be funded by the Federal Department of Transportation.

Reporters from the local newspaper, *The Clermont Clarion*, were trying their best to out-scoop reporters from the big city of Atlanta, reporters already encamped at the local court house, rummaging through real estate records, searching for clues about the identity of the backers of the new addiction center, a clinic that threatened withdrawal of federal funding of programs at major hospitals down in Atlanta.

Meanwhile Tom Owens was living incognito with his aged parents in a small middle Georgia town. He was directing construction of his new privately owned medical center in Clermont through his proxy project manager, Billy Bob Bouchard, a lay Christian preacher, a retired World War II B-29 pilot and an experienced building contractor from Alabama. In the day-to-day construction decisions Billy Bob was highly visible in Clermont. He was, however, careful to keep secret the where-a-bouts of his boss.

Clermont old timers could remember Tommy Owens only as a child, son of the local Baptist preacher whose ministry was largely forgotten. Sam Smith had retired five years earlier from his gas station. The only event he could recall about Tommy Owens was his childhood penchant for inhaling gasoline fumes whenever his father came into his station for gasoline for his 1932 Dodge Sedan. This story was quickly picked up by the local rumor mill and exaggerated to the point where everyone believed the adult Doctor Tom Owens was himself a drug addict.

That rumor was true.

CHAPTER 8
DESCRIPTION OF OWENS' CLINIC

After eighteen months of construction, the new building that would house the Owens' Addiction Clinic was finally completed: the cost, 2.6 million dollars. In all this time not one single person in Clermont had seen its owner, Tom Owens. Actually he'd come to inspect construction progress many times, but always at night or in the light of day when he drove about the site in an old grey pickup Dodge truck no one noticed.

Billy Bob Bouchard had become well known in Clermont. He was always welcomed at the local lumber yard, plumbing and electrical supply depot and cement block/brick yards because all construction materials were immediately paid with cash. Needless to tell, on such days he was accompanied with two armed body guards.

Local officials in the court house also knew him since he paid cash for all the required permits such as sewer and water line extensions and property taxes. While the county itself had no building code, Billy Bob saw to it that the new building met all State codes, especially hospital building codes which were very strict.

The community was impressed as construction

progressed. The new building was a sprawling one-story complex all under one roof. The exterior was rustic fire-proof simulated logs made out of tinted brown concrete. The building configuration was like a large letter "H" with the center section serving as the reception entrance area. Each of the four wings was to contain a specialized operation related to treatment for addictions. One contained six classrooms. At the end of the east hall was a rather large amphitheater with padded desk chairs, each with a writing table that folded up into the seat when not being used. Seating capacity was approximately 100. Down in the front were several built-in teaching aids such as a motor driven large silver screen that could be raised and lowered with the push of a button on the podium down on the lower level. The instructor had easy access to green chalk boards that recessed into the walls when not needed. The podium in the center of the lecture area had other built in controls for ceiling lights and volume control for microphones.

The west wing of the "H" shaped building housed fifty small sparsely furnished dormitory rooms, each with its own private toilet facility. A south wing contained a library filled with books on addiction plus several hundred carefully selected paper back novels that had as their themes either addiction, or Christian faith, or both. Also included in this west wing was an ultra modern physical fitness room with dozens of individual exercise machines. At the end of the hall was a blue-carpeted cafeteria and dining room.

The fourth wing contained administrative offices, a pharmacy and two medical examination rooms. Next to the pharmacy was a small chapel with stained glass windows and pews capable of seating approximately twenty people. In the front was a raised platform with a beautiful mahogany pulpit and communion table. Recessed into the back wall was a baptistery filled with clear water and illuminated with recessed blue spotlights.

In the rear section of the building, the outdoor space between the two up-right projections of the "H," was a botanical wonderland with wandering gravel paths, numerous wooden benches amid carefully cultivated azalea, mountain laurel and colorful rhododendron bushes all bordered with colorful pansy and impatient plants. In the center of this verdant foliage was a small pond fed with burbling water cascading down over native rock outcroppings. In the pond were several large gold fish lazily swimming amid blossoming lily pads. The garden was the perfect place for solitary mediation about the meaning of life.

The final project was landscaping the forty acres. Luxuriant green sod was laid amid dozens of original pine trees, some large, others smaller, but decade old trees spaced among wild rhododendrons and mount laurel bushes, all carefully preserved during the process of construction. A winding black-top asphalt two-lane curbed driveway up a gentle sloping grade connected the main building with the adjacent State highway.

Six months prior to the building's completion, full-page advertisements had appeared in several national medical journals soliciting patients for the clinic. Photos of some of the leading medical and psychological experts gave credence to the quality of expertise at this pioneering Addiction Clinic. The response was over-whelming. Within six months patient capacity was filled. The enrollment cost for four months of therapy was $40,000, paid in advance and if the patient dropped out, non-refundable. This high fee attracted corporate leaders and dignitaries whose wealth was threatened by their secret addictions.

The one and only time Tom Owens was seen was in the hiring of the new director of the Clinic. This interview was done privately down in the city of Macon. The top applicant for the position was a young physician/psychiatrist named Dr. Gustav Ginther. After extensive background checks and a complete review of his resume and a day-long interview involving annual compensation Tom hired him. It was a decision he'd never regret.

After sixteen months of construction, the big dedication day was approaching. The week before the grand opening local government dignitaries accompanied with newspaper reporters and photographers were given a private tour of the facility.

After completing the tour Doctor Paige's quote in the local newspaper had a hint of sour-grapes. The quote: "This building was constructed to be a second hospital in Clermont County."

Dr. Ginther, the new Clinic Director in charge of giving guided tours of the rehabilitation facilities to local prominent citizens, recognized Dr. Paige from his brief encounter with him many years earlier. He remembered Dr. Paige as the man who'd once insulted him and refused to give him permission to tour the old Memorial Hospital. Ginther, however, treated Paige with the utmost respect. It was not Ginther's nature to be anything but kind and hospitable. Paige, of course, consistent with his narcissistic personality, never recognized Ginther, never remembered he'd previously met him.

As the day approached for the grand opening of this new facility everyone was speculating whether its owner, Tom Owens, would appear. And of course he would. Off in one corner of the forty acre campus was a small simple house built for him and his wife, the woman he'd married while living down in Macon. He moved into his new house the day after the dedication of the new addiction complex.

His return to the Clermont community would create an unsolved mystery, a mystery for conversational speculation for generations to come.

In Clermont County Tom Owens would become a tragic legend.

CHAPTER 9
DEDICATION OF OWENS'
ADDICTION CLINIC

It was one of those perfect spring days. To be exact it was Saturday, May 12, 1968. Looming fifteen hundred feet above the campus of the new Owens' Addiction Clinic was the south ridge of the 4300 foot-high Sugar Loaf Mountain. A cloudless blue sky sharply defined the mountain's crest, it's south slope shaded with the pale-green new spring leaves of myriad oak trees, punctuated with thousands of cone-tipped perennial dark green pine trees, all intermingled with pink and red flowering rhododendrons, interspersed with muted white flower clusters of mountain laurel bushes. The temperature was a warm seventy-six degrees.

It was the day everyone in Clermont had been anticipating, the dedication of the crown jewel of their revived economy, the opening of the institution that would bring them world-wide notoriety. The previous week the local newspaper in its featured front page story announced that the president of the local Chamber of Commerce estimated the final construction cost was about 2.6 million dollars. The annual operational budget was estimated to be nearly one million dollars. At least forty local people had been hired to staff the addiction program and maintain its buildings and campus.

In front of the entrance to the administration building was a wooden platform specially constructed to highlight the many dignitaries present for the ceremony. The local Federal District congressman, Charlie Greenwood, as well as the District State Senator, Margaret Hawkins, and District Representative to the Georgia State House, Melvin Johnston, all had worked together to facilitate all the needed licenses and permits. Present, were the three county commissioners and of course Clermont's popular mayor, the flamboyant Oscar Tucker. The Georgia governor was expected to make a brief appearance, but the exact time of his arrival was uncertain. Other dignitaries included the president of the local Chamber, Charlotte Manson the top salesperson for Millennium Reality, the person who had secretly led in the acquisition of the forty acre land site. Also present were the county chairmen of the local Republican and Democrat Parties, both of whom had given their non-partisan influence to make this new mental health center free from political wrangling. Two world famous bearded psychiatrists who were generously paid for their endorsements in national advertising to recruit patients were seated on the platform, to the right of Billy Bob Bouchard, construction superintendent. His work was now completed. Last, but certainly not least of the dignitaries, was the bearded and beloved chief of staff at the revered Memorial Hospital, Doctor Henry Paige seated to the left of Billy Bob Bouchard.

Mingling before the elevated platform was a crowd of several hundred locals. A local restaurant had catered a light lunch of hot dogs with all the trimmings along with free cans of soda. In Clermont, serving free food always guaranteed a crowd. Another crowd guarantee was the presence of a blue grass band featuring the yodeling king of the Appalachian Mountains, singer Billy Jo Hargis, locally popular because he'd once sung on the stage of the Grand 'Ole Opera in Nashville.

Presiding over the dedicatory service was the new Director of the Owens' Addiction Clinic, Doctor Gus Ginther. Since arriving in Clermont two months earlier, he'd become a local celebrity. He had charisma, was a native Georgian raised on a cotton farm down near Macon, had been an athlete in his college days at Georgia Southern University, had a beautiful and personable wife, was a major in the Georgia National Guard, had three small children, two boys and a girl. Doctor Henry Paige publicly pretended to be Doctor Gus Ginther's friend and associate. However, those who knew the real Dr. Paige recognized professional jealousy on his part. He had secretly erected many barriers to exclude Ginther from ever becoming a staff physician at Memorial Hospital.

At the forefront of the crowd were several television camera crews recording this important regional event. Also prominent at the front of the crowd were reporters from the *Atlanta Journal* as well as reporters from several regional publications.

Everyone was anxious to lay eyes on the owner of this new mental health facility, the reclusive Doctor Tom Owens. No one was quite sure what he looked like. He'd once lived in this town when his father was pastor of the large Baptist Church, but then he was only a boy. Speculation was that in the intervening years he'd probably grown a beard like their beloved Doctor Paige. Reporters had arduously searched through dozens of American medical school graduate listings but no one had been able to determine where he'd obtained his M.D. degree. He was not listed in the directory of American Physicians.

One of the highlights of the dedication ceremony was the expectant arrival of the governor's helicopter that would land on the expansive campus directly in front of the Administration building. When his helicopter finally appeared in the blue sky overhead, a motorcade of twelve State Police cars simultaneously pulled into the long curving driveway leading to the front of the administration building. The "copter" hovered above its predetermined landing site, then slowly descended and gently touched down on the green grass. A cheer went up from the large crowd as the governor, his arms extended high, emerged through the "chopper's" door. He was immediately surrounded and escorted to the speaker's platform by a phalanx of muscular Georgia State Troopers.

As the Governor's entourage approached the speaker's platform Ginther, up on the platform, speaking through a microphone, revealed to the audience that an assassin threat had recently been made against the governor, thus the tight protection by State Troopers.

The Democratic Governor spoke briefly congratulating the citizens of Clermont for this marvelous achievement of securing this nationally recognized pioneering addiction clinic in their county. He congratulated its owner, Doctor Tom Owens whom the governor mistakenly guessed must be somewhere among the many dignitaries on the platform. Then after a few remarks about beautiful north Georgia, the governor apologized for leaving so soon, hurriedly left the platform, again surrounded by the cordon of burly armed State Troopers who escorted him to his waiting helicopter, which immediately ascended up into the sky and disappeared over the looming crest of nearby Sugar Loaf Mountain.

People were stunned by this sudden appearance and hurried exit of their top State Officer. As the dozen State Police cars went roaring down the clinic driveway and out onto the highway, Gus Ginther announced, "Now Ladies and Gentleman, while we prepare for the arrival of Doctor Tommy Owens, owner of this beautiful complex, Billy Joe Hargis and his Country Music Band will favor us with several musical numbers."

As the last musical note floated out over the crowd, those seated on the rostrum saw an old battered pickup truck turning off the highway and slowly entering the driveway leading up to the front of the building. The crowd of spectators watched as it stopped next to the speaker's platform. As its solitary driver opened the door and painfully emerged a hush swept over the crowd. Frenzied photographers with flashing cameras were capturing this scene. Newspaper reporters were scribbling notes. Intense television klieg lights made all shadows disappear from the person exiting the vehicle. Television cameras were zooming in on the solitary figure seen for the very first time. All observed a slender bearded man in wrinkled clothing and an ungroomed head of hair carefully ascending the four steps up and onto the platform. Warily he approached the box shaped lectern with its embedded microphone. Gus Ginther, slightly embarrassed by this unscripted scenario, backed away. For several seconds, shoulders slumped, both hands tightly gripping the edges of the lectern, Tom Owens scanned the expectant crowd gathered before him, all anxiously waiting for his first words.

Finally with slurred speech he said, "Doctor Ginther, distinguished dignitaries, ladies and gentlemen, thank you for coming to share in this dedication ceremony of my new facility for treating drug addicts." He paused, his muddled mind not sure what to say next. "My name is Tom Owens. This is my facility for curing pathetic people addicted to alcohol and other drugs. As you've observed, among those plagued with a chemical addiction, I am the most pathetic." He looked over to Gus standing beside him. "Dr. Ginther, I need help. I'll be the first person to register as a patient." He turned away, staggered back across the platform. Billy Bob Bouchard jumped up from his chair to help him down the steps and lead him to the front entrance of the building.

With cameras flashing, the stunned crowd began to murmur about the strange scene just witnessed.

Above the dissonant sounds of the crowd's babble, a small boy was heard to shout, "Daddy, was that man drunk?"

CHAPTER 10
GUS GINTHER'S OPENING
LECTURE TO FIRST GROUP
OF PATIENTS

Two days after the dedication of the completed Clinic buildings, the first group of thirty affluent addicts began checking in, each having paid $40,000 for the four month intensive recovery program. There was no money-back guarantee if their substance induced illnesses were not cured. The price for the intensive regime was cheap when the alternative of failure, disgrace, decreasing health and premature death was considered. This was a trail-blazing program for a mental and physical condition that had only recently been declared to be a disease by the American Psychiatric Association. In that context the price was worth the money.

Some patients came by chauffeured limousines, others by airport vans, a few by private airplanes to the regional airport and then a taxi for the remaining forty mile trip to Clermont. The formal program began the following Sunday.

The first five days without the patient's drug of choice

were reserved for a detoxification process to rid their bodies of the health-wrecking chemicals embedded in their body cells, especially in the brain. For some this detox time was easier than for others. A few addicts suffered extreme withdrawal pain and prolonged night-marish hallucinations. These needed continual twenty-four surveillance.

Each arrival was privately processed by the registrar, given a packet of rules for their stay, individually taken on a tour of the buildings and ground facilities, and finally, after a balanced evening meal, ushered to their private sparsely-furnished sleeping room. Here, after receiving medication to ease withdrawal symptoms (which begin about twelve hours after their last drink or cocaine fix) each patient was instructed to spend the evening in meditation and mental preparation for the following five days of detoxification. In this period each patient was instructed to carefully study the rules for their four month stay.

Every addict has different withdrawal symptoms which included flushing of the skin, headaches, palpitations, sweating, and chest pain. These unpleasant experiences provide a strong motivation for rehabilitation. During those first few nights a few experienced hallucinations and needed special restraints by attending staff members. For others withdrawal took only about twenty-four hours. Generally speaking withdrawal requires five days of constant monitoring by specialized trained sitters.

Sunday morning, at exactly seven a.m., all thirty addicts were assembled in the Clinic's small amphitheater with its six tiers of cushioned seats and writing extension desks. The mood was somber, their appearance disheveled after withdrawal misery. At the end of four months of therapy they'd be closely bonded to one another for life, but now they were strangers in a very uncomfortable seemingly threatening environment.

At the amphitheater's lower level, through a side door, the

Clinic's Director suddenly appeared. "Good morning Ladies and Gentlemen. My name is Doctor Gustav Ginther. You may call me 'Gus.'" He smiled as he backed away from the podium and added, "Within the next few days you'll be calling me other names not too complimentary but that's okay. For the next four months I'll be your mother, your father, your priest, your dictator, and any other role I need to assume to free you from the clutches of the disease that now dominates every phase of your life." He paused as he strolled away from the podium. Thirty apprehensive patients watched his every step.

"Within our group each of you has achieved success in your chosen profession, whether in business, education, or entertainment. Two of you are from nations other than the USA: one from Israel, the other from Columbia South America. You're a very diverse group."

He stopped speaking and sauntered back to the podium. "In many ways each of you is totally different from others in our group." Again he paused. To emphasize what he was about to say, he stepped around the lecture table, stopped at the front row of six men, but gazed out over the entire group, slowly making direct eye contract with each person.

"While you're dissimilar, you all have three common characteristics. It's these three characteristics we'll be dealing with in the next four months." Again he paused.

His head nodding in the affirmative, he repeated three times, each time louder, until he was nearly shouting. "You're all addicts." Pause. "You are all addicts!" Pause. "YOU ARE ALL ADDICTS!" His voice faded to a nearly barely audible whisper. "Your bodies are addicted to some chemical that's not only poisoning your body's metabolism but is also screwing up your brains, victimizing your thinking, messing up your core beliefs."

His eyes were now gazing down at the floor, hands steepled over his mouth and beneath his nose. As he walked back to the podium while his thirty uncomfortable patients shifted in their seats, eyes suspiciously glancing sideways at one another. One man appeared insulted by Ginther's accusation. He slid to the edge of his chair ready to stand up and walk out, ready to withdraw from the program and return home. For him, the previous four nights of withdrawal had been especially severe. As he thought about fleeing, he reflected on the successful business he owned, a corporation that for the previous twenty years he'd built by a life of sacrifice. He thought of its likely failure with a "drunk" at the helm. He then thought of his wife who'd threatened to divorce him if he withdrew from the program. He slid back into his seat resolved to remain. He continued listening to Gus Ginther, physician, psychiatrist, and clinic Director.

Gus seemed to be aware that some patients were on the verge of walking out. He stepped over to stand directly in front of another business man who was mentally debating whether to leave. Making eye contact but obviously sideways speaking to the entire group he added, "Not one of you consciously knows the real reason why you're an addict. Addictions have two components: chemical and psychological. Whatever, be it to the chemicals in alcohol, tobacco, or in some illegal drug, or, whether the addiction is psychological, such as to a person, to a religion, to food, or to sex, or whatever, it's the result of bad thought processing, or, as they say in AA, 'stinkin' thinkin'.'"

He walked back to resume an authoritative posture behind the podium. "We have a word you've already heard in the past five days, a word you'll continue to hear in the next few weeks. It's 'detox.' As you've already learned, its short for detoxification, and means removing all bad chemicals your drugs of choice have embedded in your body tissues, in your brain. These chemicals are poisons that will soon destroy you if not removed. You didn't become an addict over night. It'll take several weeks to cleanse your body of these toxins.

That's one reason why our program at the Owens' Clinic is 120 days in length. This detox program began that first night of your stay here.'

"About fifty years ago our nation believed the cure for alcoholism and its devastating consequences was a law they called 'Prohibition.' In 1917 the U.S. Congress enacted the Eighteenth Amendment to the U.S. Constitution. It was finally ratified by the forty eight States in 1919. It prohibited making and selling alcoholic beverages. As a social reform "Prohibition" was a total failure. Why?"

Before answering his own question, Ginther walked away from the back of the podium to stand in front of it, his left arm leaning of it. "Prohibition failed because it sought to remove the temptation. Cures are never achieved by removing temptation. Cures are achieved by amplifying the power of self-control within a person's mind. Self-control is achieved when your mind actually believes the dangers of ingesting poisons into your body, poisons such as alcohol, cocaine, and other thought-altering drugs. The real danger of such drugs is the ultimate damage to your health, or drug-induced auto accidents, or domestic violence, or impaired business activity, and or reckless sexual activity, or all of the above."

To allow his audience to reflect on what he'd just said, he moved over to the table beside the podium, sat down on it, his feet hanging over the edge, muscular arms propped against its surface.

Finally he added, "At this rehab clinic, in the next four months as you detox your bodies, I will also be probing your psyche in private counseling sessions, probing to discover the psychological 'why' for your addictions. Detoxification is not the cure. Addiction is not just a physical disease but also a malady of the mind. Without finding the psychological cause for your addiction, you'll relapse. In these sessions you'll fight me all the way because you don't want the 'why' to be revealed. Discovering the 'why' is the beginning of the cure."

He jumped off the table, stood squarely on both feet and continued, "Detoxification is the first step in overcoming addiction. The second step is overcoming denial. You're all in denial of the real cause of your addiction. Part of our therapy will be to force you to stop denying why you're addicted. When you enrolled in this clinic you took the big first step to overcoming your denial. You accepted the fact that you have a problem. But enrolling in this program is just the first step in overcoming denial. As I said, overcoming denial will be mentally painful. As this process proceeds you'll fight me all the way because you don't want the 'why' to be revealed. Entombed somewhere deep in the recesses within your brain is a secret, a secret so hidden it reveals itself only when you are sleeping, reveals itself in nightmares and dreaded dreams, reveals itself when your conscious self is turned off and your subconscious self is free to roam about within your brain." Here at the Owens' Clinic we're going to discover the "why" of your addiction.

"Third, the absolute rule here is honesty in everything we say, think, or do. There's a saying in drug therapy that the most honest person you'll ever meet is a recovering addict." He emphasized the word "recovering."

"There's another truism in rehabilitation therapy. 'All addicts in denial are chronic liars.' As an addict you've perfected the art of deceit." Again he paused to allow what he'd just said to sink into the attentive minds of the patients seated before him. He repeated, "Here at the Owens' Clinic complete honesty is the rule."

He then added, "Most addictions are multiple. In the next few days the first battle many of you will fight will be to stop smoking, whether its cigarettes or cigars." He smiled as he added, "There will be no dipping snuff or chewing tobacco. This is a tobacco-free facility. Break this rule and you'll be given two warnings. The third time, it'll be expulsion from this program and there will be no rebate of the dollar tuition you paid to be here."

He walked over to the first tier of seats, walked down the row, stopping before a middle age man. Smiling he said, "Good morning. What's your name?"

"Tim Harris." The man nervously readjusted himself in his seat.

Still smiling Gus said, "People who smoke are not able to discern their own stinky body odor, but non-smokers can." He paused for effect and then said, "I smell tobacco emanating from your body." Again a pause before he added, "This morning, you secretly smoked a cigarette just prior to entering this arena." The man lowered his head, nodded in the affirmative. His face showed remorse. Gus added, "That cigarette was your last smoke for the remainder of your life."

Gus took a few more steps over several seats. He stopped before an attractive woman in her mid-forties, the addict from Israel. "Hello. Are your accommodations here at the Owens' Clinic okay?"

"Yes."

"And what is your name?"

"Madeline Cohen."

Without hesitation, Ginther asked, "When did you smoke your last cigarette?"

Looking him straight in the eye, she defiantly replied, "It's none of your damn business."

"Wrong! That *is* my business." He was smiling, "For you, quitting will be difficult. Denial is a monkey on your back." The smile disappeared from Gus Ginther's face.

As he walked back to take a position behind the podium, he shouted, "We will be dividing up into six small groups with five in each group. Each group will be identified by the first name of the group leader that you choose. Every three weeks groups will be re-shuffled. Each person within your group will begin each session by giving a personal testimony about his or her addiction. Two rules must be observed. No last names are to be used. Second, you will begin each testimony with the words, 'My name is whatever and I'm addicted to whatever, be it alcohol, or cocaine, or whatever." Again he paused.

"Daily exercise is mandatory. You have a choice of spending one hour each day either in the gym where we have a large variety of exercise machines. Or, you might want to swim in our indoor heated swimming pool where attendants will monitor your exercise. Also, when you registered, you were given twelve books. Each book has a number on its spine. Before tomorrow's group session, you are to begin reading book number one, chapters' one through six. At each group session you will discuss these daily assignments."

"Meals in the cafeteria have been prepared with your health in mind. We have no finicky eaters here. You will not discard any uneaten food in the waste container. Learning to eat balanced meals is part of your recovery therapy."

As Gus continued his opening lecture, Tom Owens, seated alone up in the very back row of the amphitheater, was surprised when he'd happened to view the profile of a large burly man seated down in the first row. He was the patient from South America, the second foreigner referred to earlier by Doctor Ginther. Many years earlier this man had been a patient in Tom's Bogotá Clinic, a man he'd treated for kidney stones. Tom searched his memory for the man's name, and finally recalled it. "Carlos. That's it. Carlos Salazar." Carlos had been one of his ex-father-in-law's twenty-four body-guards.

Tom Owens slid down in the lecture hall seat while continuing to keep his eyes on Carlos. His mind was asking him hard questions. "What's Carlos doing here in Clermont? Is he still employed by my ex-father-in-law? Is he here as a spy to verify to his boss about this Clinic and its use to the Cartel?"

Buried deep within his mind was the unacknowledged secret that money he'd honestly and innocently accepted from his father-in-law to establish his addiction clinic was likely tainted. He couldn't prove Ivan Vanegas was a top boss in the Columbian Drug Cartel. He only had his suspicions, gut feelings he wouldn't permit his mind to think about. These tortuous thoughts were enough to dampen his hope for a cure from his own addictions.

Without the other patients seeing him, Tom quietly arose and slipped out of the amphitheater.

Later that morning he formally withdrew from the rehab program.

The other patients would never know that the man who owned this clinic where they would overcome their addictions would himself never overcome his.

Chapter 11
Monday Morning
Following Saturday
Dedication at Owens Clinic

The Clermont Café was always closed on Sunday. But on Monday, from the time it opened for business at six a.m. until it closed at three p.m., most mealtime conversations were about what'd happened the previous Saturday at the campus of the new Owens' Rehab Clinic out on the western edge of town.

"He was drunk," was the most often repeated phrase.

Others thought he might have been "stoned" on cocaine or "high" on marijuana.

Some speculated Tom Owens resembled the unkempt ungroomed eccentric billionaire Howard Hughes whom the national news media pictured as a recluse addicted to codeine, a pain-killing drug. Was Tom Owens another mentally disturbed person like Howard Hughes?

Many locals were aware that each morning Doctor Paige walked the two blocks from Memorial Hospital to the Clermont Café for breakfast. He always arrived precisely at seven. This Monday the restaurant was more crowded than usual. Everyone wanted to hear his interpretation of what had happened the previous Saturday. Early customers lingered longer than usual over their often refilled coffee cups waiting for him to arrive. Right on schedule Paige came through the opened glass front door and headed for his usual seat at the "Liar's Table" in the back of the eating emporium.

He'd no sooner taken his seat than a man's voice shouted, "Hey doc, what'd you think about what happened out there Saturday at that hospital for drunks?"

Paige's opinion was highly valued on every topic but especially this one. Everyone knew he was strongly opposed to the presence of this new health facility.

Adjusting himself in his seat, pulling it closer to the table, he coughed a polite cough and then politely replied, "Please don't refer to those addicted to alcohol as 'drunks.' Please show some respect for whose who are mentally ill."

"Well, what'd you think about Tommy Owens showing up at his hospital drunk as a skunk?" The faces of everyone in the restaurant again turned toward the "Liar's Table."

The good doctor gave another polite cough before looking in the direction of the man's voice over in a booth along the north wall. "Please, sir, don't refer to that facility as a hospital. This county has only one hospital and that's the one where I'm the Chief of Staff, the hospital were I delivered most of the children living in this county, the hospital where many adults in this region have been healed because of my medical skills and my staff of nurses and technicians."

Persistently seeking Paige's opinion about the big event at the Owens' Clinic, the man again yelled, "Well Doc, is Tommy Owens really a medical doctor as he claims? Or is he some kind of quack? He grew up in the Philippine jungles. Maybe he got a witch doctor license there."

There was a snicker of laughter throughout the café.

Again, all the customers were straining to hear the esteemed physician's reply.

By this time Maggie, the one waitress who worked a regular eight hour shift, was about to place a cup of black coffee on the table in front of him. Maggie was a deeply religious person, a member of a mountain church reputed to handle poisonous snakes during Sunday worship services. She sometimes wore a tee shirt with the words, "Jesus Saves" printed on the back. Married three times and divorced three times, with three sons each by a different father she was, however, a good hard-working loving mother.

As she bent over to place the cup of coffee before the good doctor, he gave a quick glance at her ample chest briefly exposed under a loose fitting low neck-line yellow uniform. He politely thanked her for the coffee. As he lifted to his lips the coffee mug with the words "Marcam's Insurance Agency" etched on its side, his eyes were searching for the man yelling questions. Patrons, observing his wandering eyes, began to point in the direction of the middle aged man in the booth on the north wall.

"In my opinion, that man's medical credentials need to be investigated. Where'd he get his medical degree? It wasn't down at Emory University where I got mine. And, where'd he get the money to build that multimillion dollar facility? Business men around these parts tell me everything was paid for with cash. Jim Turpin, president of our bank, tells me none of that construction money came through his bank or any other bank in nearby county's. Something's not right out there. I'm told the IRS is investigating the source of funds for that venture."

What locals didn't know is that Paige, in the hope of getting a reward for uncovering income tax fraud, had secretly invited the I.R.S. to investigate Tom Owens and his access to big money.

A surprised murmur swept across the patrons within

the restaurant at the news that the IRS was investigating the source of the money used to build the new Owens' Clinic.

Paige followed this revelation with a statement that revealed his inner-most thoughts about the Owens' Clinic. "All I'll say further is that this county isn't big enough for two medical facilities. All that money Tommy Owens spent in building that place would have been better spent constructing a new wing on the one good hospital we already have, Memorial Hospital, a place sacred to this community, a hospital where you, Hiram, were brought into this world many years ago, a hospital where your mother, Maggie, bless her presence in heaven, took her final breath of earthly air."

Maggie smiled, appreciating this special recognition of her presence by the town's most distinguished person. She bent over the table, placed before the good doctor a blue plate on which were his usual two scrambled eggs, bacon, toast and jelly. As she did so, again her low cut uniform partially exposed two large breasts, again the sight of which did not escape Paige's fleeting gaze.

"Hiram, enough of your questions. Eat your breakfast so I can eat mine. I've scheduled a surgery two hours from now. I need to get back to my hospital. I've said all I will say about that event this past Saturday, an event that has embarrassed the entire town of Clermont." He then added, "When the Atlanta newspapers print what happened here in Clermont this past Saturday, our town will be the laughing stock in Georgia."

He'd concluded his breakfast lecture with a final thought to appease those people in town who appreciated the presence of the new clinic, "I'm not saying Tom Owens doesn't deserve a lot of praise and credit for what he's done out there, but I think it could have been done cheaper and better by adding a mental health wing on Memorial Hospital right here in the center of our town." He repeated, "This community can't afford two health care facilities."

Paige was appealing to the basic instinct of the locals who had an inbred fear of all strangers. The Owens' Clinic would bring thousands of strangers into Clermont.

A few newer residents in Clermont had already concluded that the new Owens' Clinic wasn't costing the tax payers one cent of money. As a matter of fact, it was paying into county tax coffers annual revenue of thousands of dollars. Every day local residents identified automobile license tags of visitors from dozens of states beyond Georgia, people who spent money in local business establishments, wealthy men and women considering enrolling in the Owens' Clinic, or family members who'd come to visit patients, or medical specialists wanting to duplicate in other states what the Owens' Clinic was accomplishing. The Owens' Clinic was a national model in the newly developing field of addiction recovery. Its specialized staff trained to cure those addicted to drugs, both legal and illegal, including alcoholism, was being noticed by experts all across the U.S.A.

Of course, a few Clermont County residents knew that by putting an annex on the existing Memorial Hospital, Paige would have dictated the project's progress and profited from "kick-backs" from his crony's share of construction costs.

A few insiders also knew that as Memorial's Chief of Staff, Paige had secretly blocked Doctor Ginther's application to become one of the physicians allowed to admit patients into Memorial. He'd placed so many road-blocks before Gus Ginther's application that Gus had withdrawn it. Any patient at the Owens' Addiction Clinic that became ill would have to first visit Doctor Paige's office and be admitted by him.

Nearly everyone in the county could see that two health-care facilities in the small community was the beginning of a conflict that would eventually divide the community into two groups, "locals" versus people "from off." Those connected to the Owens' Clinic were all outsiders including its owner Doctor Tom Owens and its director, Doctor Gustav Ginther.

A few more perceptive folk in the town noted that Ginther never ate meals at the Clermont Café.

CHAPTER 12
FIRST THERAPY SESSION FOR TOM

It was late Monday evening after the Saturday dedication of the new Owens' Rehab Clinic. Now sober after his weekend binge, Tom Owens, legs stretched out, was relaxed in the cushioned chair in front of Doctor Ginther's office desk. Gus had taken off his shoes, propped his feet up on a stool beside his desk. This was Tom's first private therapy sessions. He began by asking his psychiatrist, the man who was the Director of his Clinic, the man who actually worked for him, "Why am I an alcoholic? Why do I drink a poison that's slowly killing me? Who am I?"

"That's what we want to discover in these sessions together. My role as a therapist is to challenge your stated beliefs to determine if they are based on logic, knowledge and facts. In this process we'll learn who the real Tom Owens is." After a pause, he added, "Within each of our minds are core beliefs which are the template for our behavior. Some beliefs are false. Some are pure fantasies, mental constructs we've created about ourselves to cover up our flaws. Other core beliefs are half truths. Others were developed in our childhood and served us well during that formative period but as adults they're defective. Some individuals have no core beliefs and therefore have erratic amoral behavior. Many people, especially those who claim to be religious, have substituted feelings for core beliefs. Feelings are transient and easily manipulated by charlatans. Addictions hide behind our impaired beliefs. In these counseling sessions our task is to sort out beliefs based on facts from beliefs based on fiction." He paused, shifted himself in his desk chair.

"Christ was speaking indirectly about human addictions when He said, 'The truth shall set you free.' Who Tom Owens has been... is the sum of what Tom Owens believes. Who Tom will be tomorrow will be the result of beliefs modified in these therapy sessions, beliefs Tom Owens can justify with supportive facts."

He paused, again readjusted himself in his chair, then continued, "Addiction treatment has two prongs. As you already know, the first is detoxification, the removing of toxins from the body, removing chemical poisons deposited in body cells by the drugs we abused. Last evening we started that process. The second prong is psychological. This is when the therapist probes into the addict's psyche or self. This investigative process by therapists is always uncomfortable and often painful for the counselee. The sports rule, 'no pain, no gain,' applies to addiction therapy."

Tom Owens was quiet for several moments, mentally processing what his therapist had just said. He finally responded. "I frequently have bad dreams, dreams of being back in the Philippines. I'm walking on a remote jungle trail up in the mountains. My Filipino guide suddenly disappears. I don't know how to find my way home. I wander into an Igorot village. Fifty years earlier these primeval people were head hunters. I'm not sure whether they've retained this uncivilized practice. As I'm walking on a dirt path between their bamboo huts they suddenly all emerge. I'm frightened. As

I walk along the narrow corridor between these cannibalistic savages they're all pointing their fingers at me and laughing. Suddenly, I realize I'm naked. It's not my absence of clothing at which they're laughing because they too are naked. They're laughing because my skin is white and theirs is dark brown. I know I don't belong among them. I begin to run. They begin throwing wooden spears at me. One strikes me in my back. In spite of the pain I keep running. Soon I'm back in the tangle of vines and jungle foliage, lost again." He paused, obviously disturbed by retelling this frequent bad dream. "Then I wake up, sweating, scared."

"And you have this dream often?"

"Yes, about once a week, usually on Saturday night."

"Saturday? Why Saturday?"

"I don't know. It's gotten so I can't sleep on Saturday night. My escape has been several shots of bourbon. I've speculated that the cause of this dream might be that when I was a child my parents forced me to attend Sunday church services where I heard my father preach sermons on hell, where I was forced to fellowship with kids who avoided me because I was a preacher's kid. My father's sermons on hell and sin always made me feel like I didn't belong, like I was a stranger among all those righteous church people whose soul's God had saved. I felt like God didn't want me because, unlike other church members, I never heard His voice talk to me. Other people claimed to have heard God's voice talking to them, but He never talked to me."

"Tell me about those years during World War II when you and your parents were prisoners in that Japanese prison camp. Few people know that during World War II, as an American civilian living in the Philippines, you were interned in a Japanese prison camp for the teen years of your life. You never talk about those years. That traumatic experience must have had a deep impact on your beliefs, on your behavior in later years."

"Life in that prisoner-of-war camp was very difficult. Food was scarce. Sometimes the Jap soldiers that guarded the camp would severely beat prisoners for the slightest infraction of their harsh rules. We had no medicines. Our clothing had patches on patches. Many Americans died of malnutrition. But my father and mother and I managed to live through it all. The faith of my parents in the American military and their faith in Jesus Christ kept our hope alive. Hope was our most precious belief."

"Hope is a good thing."

"When the American military invaded Luzon, when we saw the Japanese soldiers preparing to execute all of us, our hope was almost crushed. But a courageous Marine battalion broke through the Japanese defense and rushed to where our prison camp was located. They saved our lives. When I was set free I weighed only fifty-seven pounds."

"After that four year ordeal, after the War ended, your parents chose to stay in the Philippines, chose to return to their mission work in Baguio?"

"Yes. I was fourteen. My parents were very dedicated to teaching their Christian beliefs to Filipinos. I'm ashamed to tell you my beliefs were not that strong. After we returned to our house in Baguio, when my parents were on trips to jungle villages, I began to smoke marijuana and drink Philippine beer. I guess I was trying to block out suppressed fears after living four years in that prison camp."

"Interesting." Gus Ginther placed steepled hands beneath his chin, pondering this disclosure from his boss. "Is that why you founded this clinic? In helping others you wanted to discover the cause of your own fears?"

"Perhaps. I've heard it said that deep within the psyche of every physician there's a drive to find the cure for all diseases so that they themselves can live forever. I'm not a psychologist, but I guess I fit that hypothesis. In the back of my mind the words of Jesus keep replaying, 'Physician, heal thyself.' Perhaps this was my motivation to become a physician."

"Tell me about your childhood, growing up as the son of a Christian minister."

"Before my parents took me to the Philippines to do mission work, because my father was a preacher, our family had lived in three different communities. We'd get settled in one town, the congregation would increase, and another church would entice my father to come to their church at a bigger salary. So we'd move and my childhood friends would disappear. When I was about six the large Baptist Church here in Clermont hired my father. Again we moved. But I continued having the feeling my life in Clermont wouldn't be permanent. I never felt that I belonged. Local kids would shun me because I was a 'preacher's kid.' They thought I thought I was better than they were."

"What'd you do? Can you remember?"

"I figured I could take one of two different courses. I could rebel against the teaching of my parents and start chewing tobacco, smoking cigarettes and drinking beer as the other boys my age were doing. Or, I could retreat into my own isolated world. About age nine or ten, I discovered an escape from my dilemma. I began sniffing gasoline fumes and discovered that I experienced a sensation that erased my feeling of isolation."

"Gasoline fumes gave you a high?"

"Yeah. Back in those days, before the War, I guess maybe gasoline had different additives than now. Then after we moved to the Philippines my feelings of isolation were intensified by living as a foreigner in a third world culture. My father had an old model "A" Ford. Each evening before going to sleep I'd secretly go out and sniff the fumes in the gas tank. As I said, after the War, I began smoking marijuana with American missionary kids whose families lived near by. In the Philippines marijuana was a cash crop grown by mountain farmers, a by-product of the "hemp" plant the fiber of which was used to make rope. Before World War II "Manila rope" was a common item sold in American hardware stores. During the War it could no longer be imported from the Philippines. Then after the War synthetic fibers replaced it. Marijuana was easy to buy in the Philippines."

"So you developed these addictions to escape feelings of not being accepted?"

"I guess. I really don't know the why."

"Tell me about your medical education. Doctor Paige is making an issue of this, saying you're not a legitimate physician. Where were you educated? I know your parents were missionaries in the Philippines. Where'd you go to school, to college?"

"As I said, my father was a professor in a Baptist Bible Seminary in the city of Bagiou, the Philippine summer capital, replacing Manila with its high humidity and unbearable heat. It's about 200 miles north of Manila on the big island of Luzon. Bagiou is in the mountains, about 4,000 feet above sea level. Therefore the temperature is always about fifteen degrees cooler than other places in the Philippines. In the hot tropical summer months fifteen degrees can make a big comfort difference. In Bagiou there's a large Catholic School named Saint Louis University. Enrollment is about 10,000 students, fine campus, teachers with high academic credentials. S.L.U. was about two miles from where we lived. Prior to enrolling in college my mother taught me using the Calvert Correspondence System familiar to many missionaries. After receiving my GED I commuted to S.L.U., made good grades, majored in biology with a minor in chemistry."

"Where'd you go to medical school after you received your bachelor's degree?"

"I applied to Chaing Mai Medical School in Bangkok, Thailand. I wanted to get away from my parent's control. I was accepted. I did my internship in Bumrumgrad Buddhist hospital in Bangkok. In Bangkok cocaine usage is rampant. During my two year residency my addiction shifted from marijuana to cocaine. While there I met a nurse from Bogotá, Columbia in South America. Her name was Marie, Marie Vanegas. Her father was a Columbian diplomat in Thailand. Later he was recalled to Columbia to serve in a top government post. She was a beautiful woman. We shared an apartment. When we weren't working we'd go back to our apartment and together snort cocaine. She was more into it than I was. Eventually I married her. Her parents enticed us to leave Thailand and come to Columbia to live and raise a family. They wanted all their grandchildren around them. They built us a splendid house within their walled compound, an area that occupied an entire city block."

"Did you practice medicine in Columbia?"

"Yes. My wife's father arranged for me to be a licensed physician there."

"What about your addiction? Did her parents approve of your use of cocaine?"

"It was no problem. In Columbia, cocaine was as easy to buy as cigarettes are here in the States. In Columbia recreational use of cocaine was as socially accepted as social drinking of alcohol is in the USA."

"So, your addiction progressed from inhaling gasoline fumes, to marijuana, to alcohol and finally cocaine."

"That's my addiction path. Recently here in the States I've reverted to alcohol."

"In Bogotá how did you finance the opening of your own medical clinic?"

"My wife's father was very wealthy and very influential in the government."

"He financed your clinic in Columbia?"

"Yes."

"After two years and a moderate lucrative practice taking care of affluent citizens in Columbia, Marie died while giving birth to our first child, a son, who also died a month later. I was heartbroken. About that time my father retired from teaching in the Philippines. My parents moved back to central Georgia. In my time of grief I sold my practice in Bogotá and moved into my parent's home in a small town down near Macon. After two years of being a widower, I married Vera whom you know. She's a fine woman, was an anesthesiologist in the regional Macon hospital. Because of my own addiction problem I began thinking seriously about establishing a clinic for those addicted to alcohol. My ex-father-in-law in Bogotá contacted me. He agreed to finance it if I'd build it. We both decided such a clinic should be in a remote region where those being cured would not be tempted with worldly things, thus Clermont."

"And that's when you began building this clinic?"

"Yes."

"And your father-in-law in Columbia financed it?"

"Yes. He put together a consortium of Columbian business men to fund it. They had connections with a large bank in Atlanta. You may have trouble believing what I'm about to tell you, but at one time, while living near Macon, stuffed in about a dozen suitcases hidden in my father's house, I had over two million dollars, all cash. From that cache I paid for every part of this clinic."

Doctor Ginther leaned back in his chair, stunned by this revelation from his boss.

"You've got a tax problem. It's no wonder IRS agents were here several weeks ago, auditing our financial records. Someone, perhaps a local Clermont banker has notified them of extremely large cash deposits by local contractors constructing these building."

"I assure you its all legal. The corporation that financed this facility is a legitimate foreign corporation that has paid taxes and reported to the IRS all cash movements."

"Are you telling me the money that financed the

construction of the buildings on this campus all came from your father-in-law down in Columbia?"

"Yes."

"And you're aware of the real possibility that all of it might be illicit drug money being 'laundered' by the powerful drug cartel in South America?"

"That possibility is why I never showed my face during construction and why this past Saturday I was drunk as a skunk. As the dedication day moved closer and closer, my feelings of alienation became stronger and stronger until it became unbearable. So I turned to that which was no stranger to me, my best friend, bourbon."

Both men were silent for several minutes. Gus arose from his chair and walked over to the large plate glass window in his office. He gazed up at the crest of the towering Sugar Loaf Mountain with its blinking red beacon light. Finally he returned to his chair, sat down and almost in a whisper said, "I'm a lowly pawn in an international chess game between the American politically correct "War on Drugs" and the powerful insidious South American drug cartel. It's unbelievable to me that it could happen here in remote Clermont, Georgia."

Head bowed, Tom replied, "It's enough to cause us both to get drunk and stay drunk."

Gus began laughing, then stopped. "You know what's really ironic about this rehab clinic?"

"No. What're you talking about?"

"I've been corresponding with the director of the federal government's Justice Bureau of Narcotics and Dangerous Drugs. Three months from now, next September when we graduate our first class of recovered addicts, he's agreed to come here. Since we're a pioneering rehabilitation drug clinic he's agreed to be our guest speaker.

"I'm impressed. I hope on that day I don't show up drunk again."

"You won't. By then you'll understand the cause of your

addiction, and will have made personal resolves dealing with your temptations to alcohol."

"You believe in your recovery program, don't you?"

"Absolutely!"

"Three months from now I'll be cured?"

"No. We don't use the word cured. We just say you'll be a recovering alcoholic."

"I'm beginning to feel good about your program for recovery."

"Good. Three months from now our Clermont rehab clinic will receive national attention for our program of addiction recovery."

Gus's comment was prophetic, but not in the way he hoped.

CHAPTER 13
CARLOS VISITS OWENS HOUSE

Tom Owens was alone in his modest house located in the northeast corner of the Clinic campus. It'd been five weeks and six days since both the dedication of his Clinic and his withdrawal from its recovery program. Vera, his wife, a trained anesthesiologist, had found work in a regional hospital in the adjacent county. She was always "on call" and subject to irregular working hours. This morning she was at work when the front door chime sounded. Inside the house Tom arose from his reading, went to see who was there. He was surprised when he saw who it was standing outside on the porch of his house.

It was Carlos, one of thirty patients at his Clermont Clinic. It was instantly apparent that Carlos didn't remember being one of Tom's patients at his Bogotá clinic. Carlos had been one of twenty-four body guards for Ivan Vanegas the top general in the South American Columbian Drug Cartel.

"Señor Tom Owens?" said the man standing outside the screen door.

Hesitantly, Tom answered, "Yes?"

"I have message to give you from former father-in-law in Bogotá." His English was rudimentary. His eyes were locked in a penetrating stare at Tom's face as if trying to remember something. After an antsy pause he continued, "Do you know name of man you called your father-in-law who lives in Bogotá?"

Since his departure from Columbia Tom had seldom mentioned his father-in-law's name, not even to his wife Vera. It was part of his past he wanted to forget. Now he realized he was being tested by this intimidating man standing just outside the screen door.

"Yes. His name is Vanegas, Ivan Vanegas."

Just saying "Vanegas" caused a shudder to sweep through Tom's body. While his Columbian wife was alive he and his wife's father had a cordial relationship. But after his first wife and infant son died, his father-in-law's attitude toward him abruptly changed. Tom Owens was no longer "family." He began to consider Tom only as a potential American business opportunity. Shortly after Tom's wife died, Ivan Vanegas had approached him with a proposal that he return to the USA and there consider establishing a drug rehabilitation clinic in a remote region. All construction financing would be provided by the Vanegas family. Only the location was undecided. After Tom described his childhood home in rural north Georgia, his father-in-law immediately approved that location.

It was the furtive financing of his Clinic that had been driving Tom into deep depression which he vainly attempted to cure with alcohol. He had his suspicions about his father-in-law's motives but didn't have the courage to ask questions. It was easier to stay partially drunk. Once ensconced in his parent's home down near the city of Macon, and as all the needed money for construction became available to him, Tom's guilt drove him even deeper into his addictive illness. Now, two years later, there Carlos stood outside the door to his house in north Georgia, a reminder of his unhappy past.

"May I enter house? I have a message from your father-in-law in Columbia."

"Come in." Cautiously Tom unlatched the screen door hook. Carlos entered. Tom invited him into the living room, gestured for him to sit down in a cushioned chair.

Being somewhat uncouth and ill-bred, Carlos got right to the point for his visit.

"The message is this. You are to hire licensed pharmacist chosen by Señor Vanegas. This man will contact you ten days from now. He will replace pharmacist now employed at this Clinic. You are not to ask questions when weekly packages are delivered to Clinic by courier." Somewhat uncomfortable speaking English, Carlos then arose from the chair. He'd delivered the message. As he was leaving, he turned and added, "l will be watching to insure you do as Señor Vanegas has instructed. No one disobeys Señor Vanegas."

Tom felt within him a surge of courage. "And if I do not do what Señor Vanegas has ordered?"

With a threatening glare Carlos repeated, "No one disobeys orders from Cartel and lives." He turned and walked unescorted to the front door, opened it and stepped out. Without looking back, he proceeded across the campus, heading for the Clinic's front entrance.

Stunned by this crypto messenger with his cryptic message, Tom stood for several minutes inside the screen house door watching Carlos walk back across the campus. He then returned to the living room, slumped down into a cushioned chair. This brief encounter with an agent of the Columbian Drug Cartel revealed the true purpose of his Columbian father-in-law's financing of his Clinic. It was to be a covert drug distribution center, perhaps for the entire southeastern USA. What could be better for illegal drug distribution than a clinic for curing drug addicts? What a brilliant plan!

Tom arose from his chair and went to the closet where

he kept hidden a bottle of bourbon. Filling a shot-glass with the golden liquid, anticipating the euphoria drinking it would bring, he was poised ready to chuck its liquid contents into his open mouth. But an impulse never before experienced caused him to slam the filled shot glass down onto the table. His fear of strangers, validated by this threatening visit of Carlos, was overshadowed by a new sensation, an inner unknown force. He picked up the glass, went into the kitchen and poured the bourbon down the drain in the kitchen sink.

Shoulders drooping and with faltering steps he returned to the living room. There lying on the coffee table before the sofa he saw his father's old Bible, its black leather cover glossy from invisible oils from his father's hands tightly gripping it for decades as he delivered countless sermons from its inspired pages. Tom sat down, reached for it, cautiously opened it, began thumbing through it. His brain was buzzing with childhood memories of his father's voice proclaiming the divine Word of God. His eyes settled on a verse his father had highlighted. *"I can do all things through Christ who strengthens me."*

For several minutes he gazed at that verse, repeating it over and over in his mind. He knew it was the core belief in his father's life.

Finally, as his eyes were filling with tears, he lifted his unfocused gaze up toward the ceiling. His mind's eyes, however, were seeing far beyond the ceiling, seeing a greater vision of what sobriety could accomplish in his remaining years of life on planet Earth. Meditating on that verse caused him to realize there was an invisible Power available to him, an inner source of strength just waiting for him to tap into, a basic truth that would change his life, change his behavior. That power was the fact that Jesus was God!

****

Ten days later a stranger appeared at the front door of the

Owens' house. He identified himself as a pharmacist seeking employment.

Tom politely told him the clinic already had a pharmacist.

CHAPTER 14
CARLOS SALAZAR'S MEETING
WITH DR. PAIGE

Office hours at the Paige Clinic were from 10 a.m. until 5 p.m. each day except Wednesdays, Saturdays and Sundays. His nurse, Gretchen Schroeder, worked each weekday from eight to five with an hour off for lunch. Paige reserved weekday mornings for hospital patient "rounds" and often minor surgeries. He once calculated that in his twenty years of practice he'd removed the appendix from at least five hundred people. Memorial Hospital had no medical review board to monitor unnecessary surgeries. He was, after all, Chief of Staff. No one doubted his diagnosis for inflamed appendences. One lab technician who happened to examine one appendix specimen surgically removed by Paige declared it healthy, not inflamed. That technician was fired the next day for using "contaminated needles" in the process of doing venipunctures.

At Memorial Hospital there was also no review board to consider complaints against the half-dozen doctors with hospital privileges. The old downtown hospital was Paige's fiefdom where his control was absolute.

It was a Tuesday, early afternoon, just after Paige returned from his lunch at the Clermont Café. As he entered the back door to his office, he saw Gretchen at her desk next to the sliding glass window which opened out to about a dozen patients seated in the waiting room, patients reading old National Geographic magazines. She silently beckoned for him to stop in the hall. She stood up, quickly walked to meet him. They both entered his office. As he was sitting down in his chair behind his desk, she was closing the door.

"What?" he said, a quizzical expression on his face.

"There's a man out in reception room who wants a private conference with you. Okay? He's definitely not local. I think he's a foreigner, perhaps from Mexico or some South American nation. Okay. He speaks with a definite Hispanic accent."

"He didn't tell you why he wants to have a conference with me?"

"No. I don't think it's a medical problem."

"Send him in. I'm curious." He stood up, followed her to the door, opened it.

Within a few minutes Gretchen ushered this stranger into Paige's office. As Paige closed the office door, he asked him to have a seat. "Why did you wish to talk to me?" said Paige as he walked around to the chair behind his desk, his eyes carefully scrutinizing this husky bearded man seated in the chair before his desk.

"I am patient at Owens' Addiction Clinic." As Gretchen had noted, he had a distinct Hispanic accent.

"I don't have any association with the Owens' Clinic," said Paige, disgust resonating within each word. "They deal with chemical and emotional addictions. My practice deals with real ailments, physical ailments." His emphasis was on the word "real."

"That is part of reason I come to you today. I am not happy with treatment I am receiving there. I have been patient at Owens' Clinic two months. They have not cured me of alcoholism." He shifted his body in the chair as he leaned forward, looking Paige directly in the face. It was a menacing glare that caused Paige to look down at his desk. He unconsciously straightened a stack of lab reports stacked on the corner.

Carlos continued. "Last week I read in *New York Times* about battle over hospitals among people here. They say you are leader of opposition to Owens' Clinic."

"Yes, I also read that news story. All in Clermont County were surprised that our local hospital squabble would appear in the pages of that prestigious newspaper."

"The pharmaceutical company that employs me has interest in failure of Owens' Clinic. My employers are secretly prepared to pay you ten thousand dollars cash if you will help them discredit and put Clinic out of business."

Paige straightened his posture in his high-back leather office chair. "You'll pay me ten thousand dollars for what?"

"My employers need help from some local person who knows region, one who knows of secure remote place where four members of our organization may hide while they prepare to discredit Owens' Clinic."

"Ten thousand dollars?" His chin dropped as his mouth slightly opened, his head jerked backward and off to the side. His eyes locked onto the face of this stranger. "Are you joking?"

"No joke. Ten thousand American. Fifty packages twenty dollar bills, bill numbers not traceable, yours if you help my employer. No one will know your role in discrediting Owens' Clinic."

Greed kicked in. Paige hated the probability that within a few years the Owens' Clinic would rival his own Memorial Hospital, perhaps even replacing it. This offer from this stranger seemed too good to be true.

"When and how will I receive this ten thousand dollars?"

"East of Clermont is State Park where your tradition says Cherokees once had village next to big river. Come to State Park one week from today, 7:30 in morning. Come alone, walk east on Blue Ridge Trail. I will be waiting about two hundred meters down trail where wooden bridge crosses Sidecut Creek. Money will be in brown brief case which I will give you."

"And all I need do is provide your four cohorts a secure hiding place within this County?" questioned Paige.

"Si. Remote place must be ready two months from today. Authorities will never make connection to you and destruction of Owens' Clinic. When I give you briefcase, you will give me map with detailed written directions showing how to find secure hiding place. It must be stocked with enough canned food for three weeks. Our people are professionals and will not be discovered by police. Your role will never be known, no evidence of your part in plan to discredit Clinic."

Paige had a too-good-to-be-true gleam in his eyes. His face brightened at this unexpected opportunity to have unknown strangers somehow destroy the Owens' Clinic.   His vanity kept him from recognizing his greed. Again, he was about to sell his integrity for money, a lot of money, tax-free money, this time $10,000 in cash.

As he gazed at this stranger known only to him as "Carlos" he felt a slight tinge of fear, as if he might be making a deal with the devil. And he had.

But the devil was no stranger to Paige.

CHAPTER 15
TOM OWENS' THERAPY WITH GUS GINTHER

After six weeks of one-on-one therapy, Tom Owens and Gus Ginther had become close friends. Gus knew such bonding violated the professional relationship a therapist should have with a patient, but the fact both men were committed to making the Addiction Clinic successful, one as its director and the other as the owner, proved too strong a force to make such sessions impartial and totally objective.

Gus became the first real friend Tom had ever had in his adult years of life. His fear of strangers had always been a barrier to anyone getting close to him. However, with Gus Ginther being the extrovert that he was, this mutual friendship came naturally.

Their therapy sessions in Gus's office were always held in the early evenings, after all other Clinic patients were in their private rooms studying their next day's assignments given them by their mentors.

Gus entered his office where Tom was already hunkered down in a heavily cushioned easy chair. As he was closing the door, he apologized for being late. "I took the afternoon

91

off and went turkey hunting with Charlie from our business office."

"Where'd you go?"

"Out in the Blackberry Mountain Forest Preserve. We saw plenty of wild turkeys but I didn't kill any. I'm not much with guns. All I shot was a blue tick hound that suddenly appeared chasing the tom turkey at which I was aiming. I never could identify whose dog it was. It ran off, wounded, into the thick underbrush. I wasn't sure but I thought I saw the silhouette of a man, but when I hollered at him he disappeared."

"You're in big trouble if you shot a mountain man's hound. Their dogs are closer to them than their wives or kids. When I was a small boy and my father was the minister of First Baptist Church here in Clermont, he conducted a funeral for one of our deacons who'd accidentally shot a mountain man's coon hound. They identified and arrested the fellow who shot the deacon, but couldn't convict him because they couldn't find a jury of his peers who'd convict someone who'd shot a man who'd shot a mountain man's hound."

"No kidding." Gus chuckled at the Tom's story. "Did that really happen?"

"That's the story. Of course the 'ole coot was producing moonshine in a still hidden up in the mountain behind his cabin. The deacon he shot was a federal revenue officer."

There was a long pause in the conversation before Gus spoke. "I did everything I could to find the dog's owner. Finally I wrote a note with my name, address and phone number on it, laid it on top of a big rock, placed a small rock on top to keep it from blowing away, hoping the dog's owner would find it and contact me and let me pay for his dog."

Gus sat down behind his desk, put his feet up on the desk's top, looked at his friend, and then commented, "You look beat, worried. What's troubling you?"

A morbid tone in his voice Tom said, "I've been contacted by my ex-father-in-law."

"You have? What'd he want from you?" Gus got up from his desk chair, walked around his desk and sat down in another easy chair opposite Tom. "How'd he contact you? By telephone? How?"

"Carlos Salazar came to my house with a message from his boss, my ex-father-in-law" in Bogotá, Columbia, South America.

"Carlos? I've wondered about him. He's not going through therapy as the others are. So, what's he want? What's he doing as a patient here? I don't have any doubt that he's an alcoholic, but I seriously question that he wants to be cured."

"I was ordered to hire a replacement for our present pharmacist, Don Millikan."

"We can't fire Don. He's doing excellent work. The patients trust him and I also trust him." He paused then added, "Did Carlos mention the name of this replacement?"

"No. He said a qualified licensed pharmacist out of Atlanta would contact me at my house within ten days and that I must hire him."

"He must be someone who works for the Columbian Drug Cartel."

"That's what I immediately concluded. Carlos also told me this new man must not be questioned when packages are delivered here to our Clinic."

"Packages? No doubt cocaine. Since the beginning they've planned that this clinic would be a distribution center for illegal drugs, probably in the southeastern States." Gus jumped up, blurted out, "What a brilliant cover-up! Distribute illegal drugs from the one place Narc Agents would never think to investigate."

"All last night I couldn't sleep, worrying about this matter. I didn't take a drink, although I did get out my secret bottle of bourbon and was strongly tempted." He hesitated, then looking directly at Gus, said, "But for the first time in my life I resisted."

Gus smiled. "I'm proud of you. You've discovered you're a child of God, a God who loves you and wants only the best for you, wants to help you overcome your addiction. That discovery will change your mental template for your beliefs and thus your behavior."

Tom's disclosure of his new source of inner spiritual strength was for Gus the ultimate reward for his work in rehabilitation. After savoring the revelation of his friend's new resolve, he added, "Did you make a decision about obeying the order from your ex-father-in-law?"

Tom squirmed in his chair, readjusted himself, and then answered, "Yes."

"And?"

"I decided that part of the cause for my alcohol addiction is fear, fear of having to take control of my own destiny. I remembered what you said in our first therapy session. You said 'A man's core beliefs are the template for his behavior.' Do you remember saying that?"

"Certainly. It's the fundamental premise for all human behavior. Stinken' thinken' is the cause of most of the problems in our lives."

"In the past few days I've been reading my Bible. I read about the apostle Paul having difficulty doing what he'd didn't want to do. He said he realized his flesh waged war with what his mind believed. Paul said the solution was to give his mind reinforcement with the Spirit of Christ. I understood that to mean that he needed a different template for his behavior, as you've said. So I decided I needed to change my template for believing. I made the decision to replace the template of self with the template of Jesus Christ." With a look of peace on his face, he added, "From now on, His law revealed in His Word will guide my behavior."

Gus straightened up in his chair, leaned forward. "You've experienced an epiphany, a spiritual conversion. That's good. Every addict needs to exchange bad beliefs for good beliefs, new beliefs that will modify behavior. Living in harmony with God's Word produces good beliefs." His voice had a ring of excitement in it.

Tom added, "I've concluded that all my past fears were caused by my lack of trust in this Higher Power, the power which I now identify as Jesus Christ."

"I think our Christian friends call your experience, 'being born again.'"

"For the first time in my life, I feel empowered. The apostle Paul referred to this power as God's Holy Spirit. I believe I'll conquer my addictions by knowing they're a chemical escape from dealing with reality. I can have God's Holy Spirit to re-enforce my spirit when I'm weak. As Paul said, 'When I am weak, then I am strong.'"

"You're going to experience physical withdrawal pains from the absence of toxic chemicals that have become a part of your body metabolism."

"I can endure that because I've discovered who I am, what I am. I'm a weak person made strong because I now rely on God's Holy Spirit to strengthen my spirit. That dependency makes me strong." He paused, gave a hint of a smile and then added, "That sounds like a contradiction, but for me it's working."

Excitement still in his voice, Gus gazed with pride at his patient as he spoke. "In the Alcoholic Anonymous twelve step program you've just taken the second step toward recovery, submission to the Higher Power."

There was a profound silence between them as both enjoyed this beautiful serendipitous moment. Finally Tom concluded, "I've discovered that the meaning of life is figuring out you're not in charge and then figuring out who is in charge." He smiled.

"What a great insight into your addiction! With your new set of beliefs regarding God and Christ, and who's in charge of your life you'll need a loving fellowship to help you sustain your new set of beliefs. Let me recommend the small Christian Church north of Clermont where my family and I go each Sunday. Each week we hear a sermon from the Bible. Each week we gather about the Communion Table for a time of self-examination and rededication. Each week we're surrounded by people who love us. That's where our souls are strengthened and our faith deepened."

Tom thought for a few moments, then replied, "Churches turn me off. I don't need one. Too many hypocrites in churches. My submission to Christ is enough to sustain my new beliefs."

"Okay. I think you're wrong, but I'm pleased for your new way of thinking." Gus thought, *Everyone needs the encouragement of a fellowship of Believers. Calling Christians hypocrites is his old fear of strangers again emerging.* "What'd you decided about firing Don and hiring this pharmacist that works for the Cartel?"

"I've decided not to fire Don."

"The Columbian Cartel believes they also own you because they provided the money to build this clinic. Have you thought about what they'll do when you disobey their order?

"Yeah. There'll be hell to pay."

There was another long silence as both men reflected on the consequences of Tom's decision. Finally Gus stood up, walked over to the large office window, gazed out and up at the flashing red beacon light on top of nearby Sugar Loaf Mountain. West of the Owens' Clinic was another mountain range behind which the sun was slowly disappearing. As it did so it projected a massive black shadow at the base of Sugar Loaf Mountain to the east of the clinic. In another few minutes this creeping shadow would make its way up to the summit of Sugar Loaf Mountain. The Owens' Clinic would then be shrouded in total darkness.

As Gus observed this prescient shadow advancing up the

mountain's slope a momentary cold shiver rippled through his body.

After several moments of contemplation, Gus turned to face Tom. "My good friend, you'll not be alone in this fight. We're in this together."

Chapter 16
Dr. Paige's Deal with Chester Howell

"Doctor, your next patient, Chester Howell, is in room three. Okay?" She hesitated before continuing. "You'd better be wearing a surgical mask when you enter the room."

"Thanks, Gretchen." He grinned. He knew what she meant.

The salt-pepper-bearded white-coated doctor, stethoscope circling his neck, walked down the narrow hall of his clinic, pausing a moment before opening the door to examination room number three. He gave a quick guttural cough, took a deep breath, threw back his shoulders, placed his left hand on the burnished brass knob and opened the door. As he stepped into the room he knew what he'd see.

Seated on the examination table was a scruffy man, about six feet six inches tall, grossly overweight. Even though inside a building he was wearing a broad-brimmed sweat-stained rumpled leather hat, faded blue bib overalls on the outside of a tattered blue denim shirt. Dirty brown rubber boots extended half way up to his knees. Dried pig dung was packed between the heels and soles. His bearded face had traces of tobacco juice stain at both corners of his mouth. Unpleasant odors wafted out from every crevice of his carcass. In order to not offend other patients in the waiting room, Gretchen had immediately ushered him into this private examination room. His fearsome deep-set dark round eyes were intensively focused on his doctor entering the room.

Others might have been afraid of this huge fierce mountain man, but not Paige.

"Chester, have you been behaving yourself since I saw you last?"

The mountain man lowered his head, his menacing eyes peeking up at the man wearing the white coat. Unafraid, Paige waited for him to speak.

"I know you done heard about how those damned revenuers dynamited my still last month. All the corn I raised in my valley patches, corn I used for making moonshine, I now have to use to slop my pigs. Cain't make money feeding pigs. I git my money making shine. My corn is mine to do what I want." He raised his head to stare into the face of Dr. Paige. "I hain't telling you anything you don't already know. Doctors know everything 'bout everybody."

"Sometimes, Chester." He paused, walked to the other side of the room, his trained eyes scanning every aspect of the huge body of the mountain man seated on the edge of the examination table. After a brief pause he asked, "Are you still living in the house your parents left you?

"Yes sir. Since pappy died five years back and my mammy died two years back I hain't moved nowhere." He raised his head slightly. "It was my grand pappy's farm, and before that his grand pappy's farm. Now it's my farm, all 800 acres. Somebody has to take care of the place. I reckon I'll stay on that land 'till I die. After that, don't know what'll happen to my land. Government owns all the rest of Blackberry Mountain next to my land. One thing sure, don't want the damned government to git my land." He paused, then said,

"Maybe I'll give it to you doc, if'n you outlive me." He gave Paige a big open-mouth smile. The sight of his green-brown chewing tobacco-stained teeth caused Dr. Paige to turn his head and look away.

Paige liked what he'd just heard. He didn't expect to outlive this younger man, but one never knows when one will die. Changing the topic the doctor asked, "Chester, are you taking that medicine I gave you after your mother died of that cough?"

"Yahsur." His eyes avoided looking at his doctor who knew he was lying.

"Your mother died of tuberculosis. This medicine will prevent you from dying of the same disease."

"Yahsur. I don't wanna die like my mammy who spit up lot of blood 'fore she went to heaven. I'll take my medicine."

There was silence between the two as Paige placed his stethoscope against Chester's chest. "Take a deep breath, then hold it."

"Yahsur." Chester inhaled, turned his face away from Paige when he finally exhaled. Paige repeated the same thing again on Chester's back.

"Your lungs are okay Chester, but you must take that medicine."

"Yahsur. I promise I will. Don't wanna die like my mammy did."

There was another several seconds of silence as Paige took his pulse, then lightly felt the arteries on each side of Chester's neck.

Finally Paige said, "Chester, I have two favors I'd like to have you do for me." Noting he had the big man's attention, he continued, "I need a couple good bear roasts. Can you shoot a bear, butcher it, bring me some choice roasts?"

Making a fleeting eye contact with Paige, Chester answered, "Yahsur. I can do that for you. But it's a gitting harder and harder to find a bear to kill. Those damned government rangers are a gitting to be every place. If'n they keep troubling me on my land, I'll shoot'em. Haint scared of 'em. Last week I sic'ed one of my blue tick hounds on 'em when they come sneaking up behind my house. They shot at my dog, 'ole Blue, filled his rump with buckshot, they did. Tried to kill him, they did. Nobody shoots my dog and lives. If'n that damned ranger what shot my dog ever sets foot on my property 'gin, he's a dead ranger. Hain't scared of 'em. My land is my land. Don't belong to no damned government." His voice was elevated.

"Calm down, Chester. You must not say such things. There's a law against shooting people, especially government rangers."

This time he looked Paige directly in the eyes. "If'n they take what's mine I'll shoot 'em. I hain't scared of 'em."

"I know you aren't, Chester."

"What's the second favor I can do for you doctor Paige?"

"I have four friends coming to visit me in about five weeks. They'd like to do some turkey hunting up in the area where you live. Isn't there an old cabin about a mile south of yours, under that high cliff at the base of the north slope of Blackberry Mountain?"

"Yahsur. Nobody's lived there for years. Nobody knows who built it. The Park Rangers don't even know its there."

"Can you put some blankets in it, put some canned food in it, put one of your kerosene lamps in it, fix it up so four of my friends can live there for about three weeks? I'll give you money to buy what's needed."

"Yahsur. I can do that. I'll have it all ready in a week. I'm glad I can do something to help you. You've done so much for me and my mammy and pappy. I'd do anything for you, since you done come to my house to doctor my pappy when no one else'd come, saved his life after he done almost got his foot cut off in that bear trap when he done got careless.

Two years back you came to my cabin to doctor my mammy fore she died."

There was a pause as Paige's eyes scanned Chester's appearance, skin color, weight, posture. "Chester, could you get the roast to me by next month?"

With an affectionate gaze, Chester replied, "Yahsur. I know whar there's a bear den up on my side of my mountain. It's a bear the Rangers hain't never tagged. It'll be yourn next month."

"Thanks Chester. If you bring me a couple roasts, I won't even charge you for today's visit to my office." He smiled at the mountain man, then slapped him on the back as he said, "Now what brings you to my office today? What's ailing you? Are you sick?"

The big man stood up and pulled down his overalls, revealing redness on the inside of both legs. "I got this hurting itch here in my crotch. It's a spreading down my legs, gitting redder each day. Cain't hardly walk. Can you help me git rid of it?"

"No problem, Chester." Paige reached around to a medicine cabinet, unlocked it, opened it, took our several tubes, handed them to his patient." Here's some salve. When you arrive home rub this on your legs. Do it again every four hours. Tomorrow your soreness will be gone."

"What'd I owe you, doc? I always pay my debts. Don't owe nothing to nobody."

"Chester, you're like a son to me. You don't owe me anything. Just bring me that bear meat in a month, and get that cabin ready. Here's two one hundred dollar bills to buy the needed supplies."

"You got it doc."

"One more thing I want you to remember."

"What?"

"Don't tell anyone about the favors I've ask you to do for

me. It'll be our secret. You know how the government likes to meddle in matters that they got no business doing?"

"Yeah. I hate them damned government rangers."

"So do I, Chester. Your great grandpappy and my great grandpappy fought those damned Yankees who wanted to take our land, fighting in the war 'tween the States. That dammed Yankee government has no business meddling in our lives."

"Yeah. We don't need 'em. We take care of ourselves." He paused. "I'll fix that cabin right good and bring you that bear roast soon as I can find one to kill and butcher."

As Chester walked out of the examination room, doctor Page muttered to himself, "That Owens' Clinic won't last out the year."

CHAPTER 17
ASSASSINS ARRIVE

Twenty-one miles west of Clermont City was a nearly inaccessible wooded area known as Blackberry Mountain Forest Preserve. This twenty-five square mile region is heavily forested with majestic virgin seventy foot high Carolina hemlocks, towering 300 year old white pines, and huge one hundred year old sprawling oaks. Beneath this ceiling of dense foliage, down on the forest floor, filling in spaces where only limited shafts of the sun's rays are able to pierce the canopy are tangles of blackberry bramble mingled among century old rhododendron shrubbery and mountain laurel bushes. It's a nearly impenetrable jungle.

It was dedicated nearly a century ago as a National Park, an example of the original virgin American forests. Not even the Georgia State Forestry Department knows much about the area. In its many valleys between lush mountain slopes flow countless streams of shallow crystalline water over and around smooth massive weathered boulders and glistening gravel. Where these streams spread out on valley floors swim swarms of foot-long trout. This pristine territory is the perfect habitat for mountain lions, black bears and their dens, deer, wild turkeys, feral pigs, and scores of other native animals and birds.

A few century-old logging trails have made limited parts of this remote region barely accessible to modern four-wheeled vehicles rugged enough to crawl along on its difficult bumpy terrain. Over one of these rutty trails a battered four-wheel Jeep slowly made its way up steep mountain slopes, forging shallow creeks, bouncing over large rocks, eventually arriving at an abandoned deer-hunter's cabin in a small clearing at the base of a mountain cliff that arched over it keeping the cabin invisible from the air.

The driver parked the Jeep behind the cabin, under the narrow cramped overhang of the mountain's cliff. A tall slender man in camouflaged clothing got out, stretched his arms after a rough bone-weary one hour trip, walked around to the front of the hunting lodge, walked up the decrepit wooden plank steps to the porch, opened the rickety plank door and disappeared inside.

A half hour later another vehicle, this time a rusty green and brown four wheel drive pickup truck, common in the region, drove up to small clearing, parked in front of the cabin. Three men dressed in hunter's camouflaged apparel got out, rifles in hand. They were crudely greeted by the first man who'd heard their truck drive into the small clearing. He stood on the porch, rifle in his hands. There was no happy recognition of the others. It was obvious they were long-time associates. All four entered the cabin where a fire started by the first man was blazing in the stone hearth. In this cool mountain air its crackling warmth felt good as they stood with their back sides in front of it, gazing about this dwelling which they would occupy for the next fifteen to eighteen days.

The cabin's interior was remarkably clean considering it had been unoccupied for several decades. It was obvious to the men someone had prepared this place for their occupancy. In the center of the room was a bare plank table surrounded by four sturdy wooden chairs, a kerosene lamp in the middle of the table. Neatly arranged on the north side of the room opposite the one door were four portable cots containing air mattresses on which were stacked blankets and pillows. On the room's south side was a kerosene stove, a crude cupboard containing a few cups and dishes, basic cooking utensils, a large cooler-chest filled lined with a tough plastic bag capable of holding a gallon of pure water from the spring-fed stream flowing out of the cave behind the cabin. A primitive stove sat next to a shelf stocked with enough canned food to feed four hungry men for a month.

About a mile distant, as the crow flies, was a similar crude cabin in which Chester Howell lived.

The men spoke in their mother-tongue, Spanish but occasionally in English. Their guns were not for hunting wild game but carefully crafted sniper rifles.

It was late in the afternoon, one week before the graduation ceremony of the first class of thirty recovered alcoholics at the Owens' Addiction Clinic. The cabin occupants were seated on the edge of its porch smoking cigarettes. The largest asked, "Tomorrow, two o'clock, we secretly meet Carlos at the appointed place? He will give us details about targets?"

"Si," said the tall slender Columbian. His brow wrinkled as he observed the truck parked a few feet in front of the cabin. "We must not have truck remain here after we complete assignment. It would be visible in air search for us. Not space to park it behind cabin, under cliff."

The other men nodded their heads in agreement.

The tall slender Columbian said, "We will leave it at base of mountain where we shoot. When discovered, no one can trace it to us."

The smallest said, "Parked truck will mislead police in search for us."

"Si," said the man with the heavy beard. He added, "Guns and ammunition ready."

"Will Carlos be sober?" said the largest man.

"After four months living in luxury in that hospital he will be sober." The other two laughed.

"Carlos loves liquor more than women," said the man with the heavy beard. They could not imagine Carlos without a glass of Pulque or Tequila in his hand.

The smallest of the four turned to gaze off into the nearby woods as he mused, "After we do it, we then return here?"

The tall slender man responded, "Si. We return here, hiding, then begin long journey back to Bogotá and our women."

"After we do it, the man picks us up, the man who has arranged our cover-up travel back to homes in Columbia?" asked the big man.

"Si," said the tall slender man.

"How long will we stay here after we kill?" said the man with a long scar across the right side of his face.

"No more than two weeks," said the tall slender man.

The bearded man, with a sudden spastic movement of his hand, snatched a four-winged dragonfly hovering in front of him. As he slowly opened his fist, with stubby fingers on his other hand he pinched off its two back opposing wings, then tossed it up into the air. With its two remaining wings it flew in uncontrollable ever-tightening circles until it smashed into a porch post, fell to the earth where it continued a convulsive spinning.

The four men watched, amused, fascinated, laughing at this normally airborne creature, a master of flying and hovering, now in the throes of death. The big man arose, stepped over to the crippled insect and with his foot squashed it into the ground.

The tall thin man said, "One week from today, comes the reason for our being here. Tomorrow we survey our positions on Sugar Loaf Mountain."

Chapter 18
Tom's Therapy Session the Evening before Graduation Ceremony

During the first four months in the day-to-day operation of Tom's Rehab Clinic, his concern for its success caused him to maintain a low profile. He'd withdrawn from all lectures. He was not participating in group sessions. His physical presence was seldom visible among patients, staff, and especially in the local community. His rebound from previous chemical abuse was being guided in private therapy sessions with Doctor Ginther. They were close to discovering the psychological cause of his addiction. His core beliefs about life, his concept of self, and his defective theology were gradually being modified. He was close to rejecting the love of his life, alcohol.

Four months earlier, after his first therapy session, Gus had observed a slight jaundice in Tom's skin. He'd scheduled Tom for a complete physical examination at a diagnostic clinic in Atlanta. When lab reports came back Tom learned he was dangerously anemic. Alcohol interferes with a healthy liver filtering out toxins from the blood which is continually passing through it. Tom's prognosis was not good.

Now it was the evening before the long anticipated day when the first group of patients would be formally discharged and sent back into the real world of sobriety. In one of his final therapy sessions, as Tom sat in the chair across from his desk, Gus said, "Tom, this evening I want to tell you two things that I've learned about your addiction. Four months earlier I sent you to an Atlanta lab for blood tests to determine the condition of your liver. Last week when we met I detected an increased yellowish tint in your skin. I've arranged for you to return to the Atlanta lab for further tests to measure the increased blood levels of enzymes related to dying liver cells. Fifteen years of hard drinking has severely damaged your liver."

"You're right. I also have observed an increase in my jaundiced condition. Tell me the date and I'll make it the top priority in my schedule." He took out a pen and reached for a note pad on Ginther's desk. "What's the date?"

"This coming Wednesday, September 26, at 10 a.m."

"Got it. You mentioned a second thing you wanted to tell me. What?"

Gus readjusted himself in his desk chair, the palms of his hands joined together under his chin, like he was beginning a prayer. "I've been giving your addiction much thought, researching journals and so on. From what you've told me about your life in our previous sessions, I believe I've determined the psychological cause of your alcoholism. Other than your possible liver problem, which concerns me, there's nothing wrong with your mind. Your problem is primarily cultural. To put it in simple terms, you have a fear of strangers. It's an anxiety that developed in your very early childhood."

Gus paused briefly, glancing over at Tom. "In our cognitive development, at about age twelve months, infants learn to differentiate caregivers from unfamiliar people, or strangers. Infants love playing peek-a-boo, a game in which they learn that fear is easily overcome. Later, children go through a shy period when they withdraw from strangers, their parents being their comfort zone. Under normal circumstances this transition from fear to acceptance of strangers comes easy when there's no interruption in the daily family surroundings. If this continuity of a friendly environment is broken by continual change in familiar faces such as frequent family moves into different cultural neighborhoods, the child at about the age of eight or nine may, but not always, may seek emotional comfort in chemicals such as the nicotine in tobacco, or alcohol, or some other chemical such as the vapors from model airplane construction glue, or in your case fumes from gasoline."

"You're saying my problem is not mental or genetic, but cultural?"

"Yes. A person suffering from xenophobia is unaware of his or her fear of strangers. In some cases this unrecognized fear manifests itself in violence. After the American Civil War, in the southern states it was this fear of liberated slaves that formed the psychological backbone of the Klu Klux Klan, an organization that intimidated Blacks. In our time we see this emerging fear in our national attitude toward illegal Mexican immigrants. It wouldn't take much to spark this latent fear into national violence.

"Interesting." Tom moved forward to sit on the edge of his chair. "You think my fear might lead me into violence?"

"No. Not in your case. There's a secondary form that's cultural in its origin. It rarely leads to aggression, but turns a person inward into social isolation. This cultural form often leads a person to seek comfort in chemicals such as alcohol or some other drug."

"That fits my addiction. I'm most happy when I'm by myself. Association with people has always frightened me.

In social situations a drink of an alcoholic beverage alleviates my fear of successful interaction with people. A daily shot of whiskey got me through my internship where I had to interact with hundreds of Thai people, strangers."

"This cultural fear of strangers is caused by external forces, such as the interruption of the normal expansion of a child's worldview, such as the family that frequently moves in the person's childhood and the resulting trauma of building new relationships."

"Is this fear common in our society?"

Gus thought for a few moments. "Well, no. Most people in their childhood development have the security of gradually seeing new faces, having his or her world slowly opening up, having neighborhood playmates at ages of four or five. These expanding relationships continue with early school experiences. They maximize as the child moves up through the sequential levels of elementary school, high school, and on through college where many friends or at least acquaintances accumulate."

"That makes sense to me. As a son of a minister I remember at least three family moves in the first nine years of my life."

Gus inquired, "I need to know more about your life in Bogotá. How extensive was your medical practice there? What kind of physician were you? Did you have many patients? Did you have any close Columbian friends?"

"No. In Bogotá I had a family practice. My practice consisted of routine medical problems, vaccinations, colds, sore throats, etc… you know the typical daily case load. If a family doctor here in the States has one complicated medical case in a week he has a normal practice. My practice was not what a good physician here in the USA would consider difficult. Most of the elite families would come to me for common ailments easily cured with routine medicines. Many patients were from my wife's family, which, by the way, was very large. My wife's father had twelve sons and six daughters.

Eight sons were from his first mistress, two by his second, two by his legal wife. By his legal wife he had eight children. All adult sons and daughters had large families." He stopped talking, momentarily glancing up at his therapist, smiling he said, "I guess it could be said I truly had a 'family' practice."

His interest piqued, Gus leaned forward. "You're saying your medical practice in Bogotá didn't deal with complicated cases?"

Tom fidgeted, straightened in his chair as he defensively replied, "A good RN here in the States would have been very successful dealing with my patient load in Bogotá. Cases I couldn't diagnosis I'd refer to specialists up in Miami. Most of my patients had access to private jets. Many would fly to Miami every few months just to shop, and while there check in with medical and dental specialists."

"Why'd you drop out of our first group of patients here in the clinic you own?"

"On that first day I discovered, to my complete surprise, that one member of the class was one of my former patients in Bogotá." He stared out the window, not focusing on anything except the nearby mountain. "He was one of my father-in-law's two dozen body-guards. He's the same man who came to visit me at my house last month. As we both now know, his name is Carlos, Carlos Salazar."

"That first day in our orientation session you were afraid to confront Carlos. Why?"

"Yes. That first day I had this instant delusion he was a spy sent by the Columbian Cartel." He paused and then added, "Back then I thought I was just paranoid. Now I know I wasn't."

"Because your father-in-law financed this facility you now believe he has ulterior motives for this Clinic?"

Tom again shifted his body in the chair, crossed his legs, his gaze down at the carpeted floor. "That's my fear. Last month it became reality when Carlos came to visit me at my house with the message from Ivan Vanegas to hire a new pharmacist that works for the Cartel."

Gus wondered if this conversation was moving into a realm he didn't want to probe. "If your fear is rational, we need to be alert for the next move by the Cartel to use our clinic for reasons only they know, reasons we can only guess."

"Yeah. Late last night when everyone was sleeping I went into our registrar's office to check enrollment of patients already signed up for the next four month session. Our rehab program is attracting attention among national celebrities. We've enrolled two prominent Hollywood movie stars and a leading Rock band leader. We've also enrolled more foreigners: two Israeli's, three from England, one from France." He paused, then added, "...but none from Bogotá, Columbia."

"I'm not certain Carlos was ever motivated to seek a cure for his addiction to alcohol," added Gus. "In my counseling sessions with him, he resists telling me the truth about his alcoholism."

"From the clinic's daily log I've learned that in the past four months Carlos has checked himself off campus at least six times and each time he stayed off-campus for sometimes half a day."

"In these remote mountains where could he go?"

"Two months ago he had a local taxi from town come out here to pick him up. Since this small town has only one taxi I checked with the driver. He told me he first took him to visit Dr. Paige at his office. A week later the taxi driver took him to a State Park a few miles east of town. There he waited for a half hour while Carlos walked alone down a densely wood trail carrying a leather briefcase. When he returned the briefcase was missing. The driver then drove him into town, to the Clermont café, where Carlos had coffee with someone never before seen by the cab driver who knows everyone in Clermont. Later he brought Carlos back to our campus."

There was a moment of silence before Tom added,

"I checked with our campus security officer who tells me that this past week Carlos was transported somewhere by a middle aged bearded man driving a brown beat-up pickup Dodge truck."

Gus mused, "We may have a problem more serious than your addiction."

"Yeah." He was quiet for several seconds and then added, "In therapy the counselor is supposed to disentangle and extract the patient's fears, not become infected with the patient's fears."

Gus gave a half-hearted laugh. "You're correct. The therapist shouldn't be infected by the patient's fading alcohol-induced delusions."

"But what if the patient's delusions are reality?"

CHAPTER 19
SATURDAY, SEPTEMBER 21, 1968,
GRADUATION DAY AT THE
OWENS' CLINIC

It was the big event for which many in Clermont had been waiting, the ceremony that marked the completion of the first four month rehab class at the Tom Owens' Clinic. Because of the program's rigors, four of the original thirty patients had dropped out. However, twenty-six survived and now had control of their addiction. They all understood that for the remainder of their lives they'd be "recovering" and never free from their temptation. One recovering patient testified, "Every alcoholic stops drinking. It's nice to be alive when it happens."

They not only had been detoxified of addictive chemicals that previously hindered normal body metabolism, but now had integrated into their psyche a mental strategy for dealing with their compulsion.

The structured recovery model used by Doctor Ginther had proven to be 87% effective, a high figure worthy of future fine-tuning. As a premier treatment center in its field of addiction rehabilitation, the Owens' Clinic could expect to receive not only national and international recognition but also federal U.S. funding.

Present on the platform this day were twenty-five men and one woman. Never had they looked healthier. All were proud of this victory except Carlos Salazar who was mentally counting the hours until he could find a tavern.

Also seated on the platform were several local dignitaries including Clermont's mayor, the three county commissioners, and of course Doctor Paige, beloved community physician and Chief of Staff at "the other local hospital."

U.S. Marine General "Hap" Edison (Retired), Director of the newly created Bureau of Narcotics & Dangerous Drugs (BNDD), closed his twenty minute speech with these words: "In conclusion, let me sum up what I've said here today. The solution to our nation's drug problem involves four steps: First, interdiction of illegal drugs being smuggled across our borders. The South American cocaine cartel is an ever-expanding international business structure with an annual estimated budget of over 800 million dollars. We'll never totally stop the flow of illegal drugs into our nation, but we will greatly reduce its flow, thereby reducing profits of those who produce cocaine. As the cost of an ounce increases, the result will be a decline in the number of recreational users who no longer can afford it. Only those deeply addicted will continue to find ways to purchase the drug.

"That first step leads to the second. This is the treatment and recovery of those already addicted. At the present time we have no good model for recovery from the disease of drug dependency. You here at the Owens' Clinic are pioneering one treatment model. Out in California another treatment model is being explored. The Alcoholic Anonymous program developed in 1935 uses a "Twelve Step" model which seems to be effective. President Lyndon Johnson has led in shifting a portion of national funding from law enforcement to treatment. That's a good step. I've encouraged Doctor Ginther to apply for the Owens' Clinic to receive federal funding. Such funding will reduce the future cost per person enrolled in this clinic. Vietnam is providing multitudes of discharged military veterans addicted to drugs.

"The third step in our war against illegal drugs involves enforcement on both the national and international level. On the national level our federal government is considering making cocaine a controlled substance and creating a Drug Enforcement Agency. This federal agency will have congressional-given powers to seize property used by illegal drug merchants, arrest dealers and sentence them to long prison terms, finance undercover informants, and destroy money laundering schemes the Columbian Cartel uses for converting illegal profits into legitimate business enterprises within the USA.

"And finally, the fourth step involves education. The purpose of our war on drugs is to make the use of illegal drugs socially unacceptable. Instead of being glamorous, public opinion needs to view addiction for what it really is, a deadly disease. Our government has allocated several million dollars for use by the American media to change public perception about the dangers of drug usage.

"That ladies and gentlemen is our national program: Interdiction, Treatment, Enforcement, and Education. I congratulate Doctor Owens for his vision in creating this rehab clinic. I congratulate Doctor Ginther for his deep insights into the causes of addiction. I congratulate all twenty-six of you men and women who've completed your long and difficult recovery program to the happy life of sobriety. Thank you for listening."

Polite applause rippled across the audience of approximately two hundred people seated on metal chairs on the grassy lawn. His listeners included family and relatives of the twenty-six recovered addicts as well as local business leaders and curious locals who were present for the free food and music.

Also in the audience were several newspaper reporters and photographers. Even though the federal government's drug czar was the guest speaker, the occasion was not considered important enough for Atlanta television stations to send crews to record the event. Only one TV crew was present, reporters from a small television station serving north Georgia's sparse population. They were about to video record the scoop of the year.

General "Hap" Edison stepped back from the solid oak podium with its embedded microphone mounted on a shiny chrome plated steel post. He took his seat off to one side of the chair in which Gus Ginther had been seated, a chair just to the left of the podium.

As Gus stepped up to the microphone, the twenty-six recovered addicts spontaneously arose from their chairs and began to wildly cheer and applaud. Within seconds the entire audience seated on the lawn before the platform was on it collective feet and applauding him. It was obvious Gus Ginther was a popular man in Clermont. Local dignitaries, including the Clermont mayor and County Commissioners also saw Ginther as a rising popular personality that would bring their community much national attention and outside sources of income.

Doctor Paige representing "the other hospital" in Clermont County reluctantly arose from his chair and politely applauded. Within his soul there was resentment and jealousy coupled with the clairvoyance jealousy often induces. He foresaw his own popularity diminished, and even worse, the future of the old Memorial Hospital doomed to extinction. This new mental health facility would undoubtedly expand and someday become a regional hospital with all of the facilities in the healing domain. In the back of his mind he was wondering about that pharmaceutical company

Carlos had referred to, what they were doing to destroy the Owens' Clinic. If he'd known their plan, he'd not be up on this platform today.

"Ladies and gentlemen, we thank General "Hap" Edison for his insightful role as director of our national war on drugs." Gus turned and personally shook the hand of "Hap" Edison. Again ripples of polite applause.

Doctor Ginther turned back to face his audience. "Ladies and gentleman, it's my distinct pleasure to acknowledge the one man whose vision and organizational skills have made this Clinic a reality. He's a shy man who does his best to avoid publicity. We cannot complete today's victory ceremony without hearing a few words from the creator of this Rehab Clinic, its sole owner, my close personal friend, a man who personally shares in the recovery success of these other twenty-six recovering addicts, Doctor Tom Owens."

Again loud extemporaneous applause as Tom Owens reluctantly arose from his chair and humbly stepped over to stand behind the podium. With outstretched hands he motioned for the audience to be seated. "Ladies and gentlemen, honored patients, friends, it's my pleasure today to see the fulfillment of my dream. As you all know, I am myself the victim of chemical addiction, both to alcohol and formerly to cocaine. But today's the happiest day of my life. Because of the therapy insights of Doctor Gus Ginther and in the past four months of my counseling sessions with him, I, along with these twenty-six graduates, consider myself to understand the cause of my addictions. Because of Doctor Ginther's emphasis on changing my core beliefs, the template for all human behavior, my life has been modified to the point where I am now able to reject my former compulsions for psychoactive drugs."

He turned, walked over to Gus who stood up. Both men hugged, concluding with two pats on the backs of the other. As the audience spontaneous applauded, Tom turned back to stand behind the podium. Again everyone grew quiet. "Not only has Gus been my personal therapist, he also has become my close personal friend."

Just as Tom Owens was emotionally choking up, as he again turned to thank Gus Ginther and acknowledged his spiritual debt to him,… it happened!

CHAPTER 20
FOUR ASSASSINS PULL TRIGGERS

While the graduation service at the Owens' Clinic was in its early phase, four men dressed in camouflaged fatigues were driving their battered four-wheel drive Jeep over isolated back trails up to the summit of Sugar Loaf Mountain. Their second vehicle, an older dented-metal camouflaged green-and-brown pick-up truck, they abandoned in a rock quarry at the base of the Mountain. The plan was that its later discovery would misdirect law authorities searching for them.

The Jeep stopped at the edge of the south slope of the ridge. Its occupants got out and immediately began a short descent to a flat rock outcropping just a few feet below the mountain's summit.

The four were familiar with the terrain. In the previous three days they'd explored this area as presumed hikers carrying walking sticks. This time they carried not walking sticks but specialty rifles concealed in ponchos.

It was Saturday, September 21, 1968. The time, 1 p.m. The temperature, a mild 72 degrees. The sky was clear with a slight breeze. Deciduous trees on the mountain's south slope had already dropped their summer leaves making the granite rock ledge on the cliff's ridge more visible. Trees lower on the mountain, oak, maple, and aspen, still retained their yellow and crimson leaves. Intermingled on the mountain's forested south slope were scatterings of tall pines with conical tops and green needles. All blended into nature's spectacular early autumn display.

The outdoor ceremony at the Owens' Clinic was clearly visible less than a quarter mile below. The front lawn of the Owens' Clinic with its assembled crowd was in the closing phase of its formal graduation celebration.

The four professionals assumed belly-down sniper-sprawl positions. Each Columbian propped his M40A1 bolt-action rifle against the top of a small boulder so as to give him a steady aim and accurate shot. A few days earlier, on one of their reconnoiter excursion, a laser rangefinder had given them the precise distance to their targets. Each now adjusted his Redfield 3-9 scope, taking into consideration the altitude of the ridge, air density, temperature, slight wind speed, and bullet drop at this distance. Each inserted into his rifle's breech one high-velocity cartridge precisely filled with 168 grains of gun powder.

They were ready to fulfill their mission.

Each pressed his cheek onto the indentation of the personalized carefully crafted fiberglass gun stock. Each lightly placed the ball of his index finger on the trigger to avoid jerking the gun sidewise in the slightest amount. In the crosshairs of their scope each man saw his previously assigned target.

"?Estás listo," shouted the largest assassin. In the cross hairs of his telescopic gun sight was the chest of "Hap" Edison.

"Preparado," shouted the assassin with the bearded face. In the cross hairs of his telescopic gun sight was the chest of Gus Ginther.

"Preparado," shouted both the tall skinny assassin and

the short Columbian. In the cross hairs of his telescopic gun sight was the chest of Tom Owens.

"Preparado," shouted the assassin with the long deep scar across his right cheek. In the cross hairs of his telescopic gun sight was the chest of Doctor Henry Bartram Paige.

Snipers have a motto: "One shot. One kill." If the first shot misses, the targeted victim takes cover and attempts to locate the position of the shooter.

Today it would be four simultaneous shots, four kills.

"Pull!" shouted the tall skinny assassin. Each marksman took a deep breath of air, held it as he squeezed the trigger. Four steel-tipped lethal missiles were propelled toward their targets on the speaker's platform at the Owens' Addiction Clinic.

One second later, four people on that platform would be dead, that platform on the front lawn of the Owens' Clinic, that platform with its seated staff, graduates, distinguished guests, and prominent speaker!

CHAPTER 21
FOUR BULLETS STRIKE FOUR TARGETS

The simultaneous cracking salvo of four high-powered rifles firing, four bullets traveling at super-sonic speed two seconds ahead of impacted air waves, four lethal projectiles struck before their sound was heard by the assembled audience at the Owens' Clinic.

The first struck General "Hap" Edison directly in his neck. Instantly he fell from his chair and down onto the platform's floor, flailing hands grasping his neck from which blood was spurting from the two-inch hole in his fatal wound. At that same instant a terrified audience saw a second person fall off their chair and onto the plank stage. It was the woman from Israel seated directly behind "Hap" Edison. The bullet that had pierced his neck had exited through the back of the soft tissues and entered her chest. Bleeding profusely she silently slumped over in her chair and then slid down onto the plank flooring, hands clutching her chest.

That identical moment, another bullet meant for Tom Owens scraped the steel microphone post on the podium directly in front of him, was deflected from its primary target. The assassin's aim had been ever-so-slightly altered milliseconds before the trigger had been pressed because in his telescopic gun sight the assassin saw Tom turn sideways to face Gus Ginther. Otherwise, the bullet would have hit him squarely in the heart.

The diverted bullet entered the chest and heart of one of the twenty-six graduates seated at the end of the front row. Carlos Salazar, a shocked expression on his face, reflexively gripped his chest as blood began oozing out from between his fingers, spreading out over his white silk shirt and blue linen suit coat. Within minutes he died.

A third bullet embedded itself in the thick top horizontal brace of the oak arm chair in which Gus Ginther had been seated. Had he not risen to congratulate Tom, he also would have been killed.

A fourth bullet meant for Henry Bartram Paige with his salt-and-pepper beard and bald head struck Billy Bob Bouchard who also had a bald head and salt-and-pepper beard. The assassin with the facial scar had mistaken one man for the other.

Pandemonium reigned among the crowd seated on the lawn before the elevated stage. Screams of terror blended with the discordant clanging from two hundred metal chairs toppling into and onto one another. Men and women fell to the ground in an attempt to save themselves from what they concluded would be a continuous rain of death from the south summit of the nearby Sugar Loaf Mountain.

Instantly Gus Ginther knelt down beside the Israeli woman as he attempted to stop blood flowing out from her deadly chest wound. Tom Owens, not yet realizing he'd been a primary target of the assassins, fell onto his knees beside "Hap" Edison and attempted to stop the flow of spurting blood from the General's mortal neck wound.

No one attempted to save the life of Carlos Salazar. No

one ever learned about his role in arranging for this deadly assault.

Later, in recalling the sequence of terrifying events, someone present on the platform remembered seeing Doctor Henry Paige, seated next to Billy Bob, jump off the back side of the platform, seeking safety under its thick plank flooring. Paige denied this version, claiming that he jumped off from his chair, knelt down to administer aid to the dying Billy Bob Bouchard. Fortunately for Paige, the video tape that captured the tragedy didn't include him in the footage.

That day the electronic images of the quadruple murders, electronic images recorded by the lone television crew from the small north Georgia TV station, were the major news story on all major TV stations across the USA. Their video footage of the tragedy was also seen by millions throughout Europe, especially replayed many times on Israeli television. Before the day ended, millions of people on planet Earth had heard about the massacre at the Owens's Drug Rehabilitation Clinic in Clermont, Georgia.

For the Clinic its greatest moment in achieving world wide publicity for its treatment of drug addicts was also its death knell. It was the harbinger of the termination of its recovery program. Tom Owens had refused to obey orders from the Columbian Cartel. Tom Owens was their nemesis. The Owens' Rehab Clinic could not financially survive this deadly stigma. In the minds of potential patients it was an event that might be repeated. The South American Drug Cartel had achieved its goal: the destruction of its aborted distribution center for illegal drugs throughout the southeastern USA.

Doctor Paige was ten thousand dollars richer, but terrified as he speculated the bullet that killed Billy Bob had been meant to kill him. He realized the assassins had planned to kill him because of his involvement in their violent plot. Dead men don't talk. The death of Carlos would forever seal his secret from the authorities. No one ever made the connection to his involvement in that day's terrible crime. He had some comfort knowing he couldn't be implicated for arranging a hiding place for the four assassins.

However, the deal he'd made with Carlos Salazar for the figuratively "thirty pieces of silver" would haunt him until his dying day. This fact and its associated guilt intensified his fear of all strangers. Somewhere, Paige believed, was another bullet that would at some unexpected moment take his life.

In fact somewhere in Clermont County there was a gun loaded with a bullet destined to kill him.

CHAPTER 22
THE SEARCH FOR THE ASSASSINS

Immediately following the assassination of General "Hap" Edison, Federal, State, and local governments spared neither expense nor personnel to find his killer. The death of the three other victims was seemingly unimportant. The logic was that finding the slayer of "Hap" Edison would lead them to the other three assassins.

Four concurrent bullets meant four shooters. It was immediately apparent that the same bullet that killed "Hap" Edison also killed the woman from Israel. It was meant to kill only "Hap" Edison. The death of the Israeli woman was collateral.

The second bullet was meant to kill Tom Owens but was deflected by the steel microphone post into the chest of Carlos Salazar. His death was obviously an unavoidable mistake by one of the assassins because of Tom's unpredictable movement.

Simultaneously a third bullet was embedded at chest level in the oak chair were Gus Ginther had been seated. It obviously was meant to kill him.

The fourth bullet, a planned hit, pierced the heart of Billy Bob Bouchard. The motive for killing Tom Owens,

Gus Ginther, and "Hap" Edison was easy to determine, but why kill Billy Bob? Investigating FBI agents never made the connection of the similarity of appearances between Billy Bob and Henry Paige. The truth they would never learn was that the assassin had made a mistake in choosing his target.

Within two hour after the tragedy the FBI, GBI, and the Alcohol Tobacco and Firearms Bureau were all present in Clermont County. Before the sun went down on that calamitous Saturday, these law enforcement agencies were swarming throughout north Georgia, southwestern North Carolina and western South Carolina in their attempt to find the assassin of the top official of the Federal Agency for Drug Control. Military and state police helicopters were flying over the hundreds of square miles of state and national forests searching for the escaping culprits. Deputies from contiguous counties set up roadblocks on every strategic intersection in and out of the region. Clermont County was in fact sealed off. There was no possibility the assassins could escape. Since the campus of the Owens' Clinic was within Clermont city boundaries, Lucas Smith, municipal chief-of-police, ordered his five police cruisers to patrol every street within the city, in this intensive effort to find the killers.

One hour after the four murders Sheriff Howard Lammars and six deputies were up on top of Sugar Loaf Mountain searching for the precise location from which the killers had fired their fatal bullets. Because Lammars thoroughly knew the terrain it didn't take him long to find the site. Four empty metal rifle casings identified the spots and the caliber of the rifles. Lammar and his deputies secured the area with yellow tape. Other deputies were stationed at the park's entrance to seal it off from curious citizens who might want to explore the killing site thus contaminating the origin of the criminal act. He also had deputies establish a one mile perimeter that included the few campers and hikers who might be in that zone. All were corralled and interrogated for possible information of what they might have seen in the previous hour. Sheriff Lammars and twelve deputies began making ever widening circles looking for evidence.

Within an hour they discovered the old battered green and brown camouflaged pickup truck in the deserted rock quarry at the foot of the mountain. It appeared it might be connected to the shooting. Tire marks indicated the truck had recently been abandoned. Deputies circled it with yellow tape fastened to nearby bushes and trees. A deputy was assigned to stand guard to prevent contamination of this possible evidence. Lammar's conclusion was that the killers were now hiding somewhere in the immediate area around Sugar Loaf Mountain.

The biggest find was the discovery of the weapons used by the killers. One deputy noted for his hunting skills observed what first appeared to be turkey scratching among ground covered leaves. Closer examination of the soil revealed it had been freshly disturbed. The deputy carefully probed into the fresh dirt with the blade of his ten inch hunting knife, felt the tip strike what he knew was metal. With gloved hands he cautiously pushed aside more leaves and dirt. About eight inches below the earth's surface the grey metal barrel of a gun appeared. With a little more digging he exposed the hastily buried rifle with its attached telescope. He whistled for Sheriff Lammars. Donning rubber gloves Lammars and his deputy carefully extracted the gun from its shallow burial hole. It was a sniper's rifle!

The find quickly led to searches for the other three. Within ten feet of the first hole three more rifles were found in similar hastily dug shallow trenches. This discovery of the assassin's weapons was a major breakthrough and gave their investigation impetus.

FBI agents from their regional Atlanta office arrived by helicopter. Unfortunately for Sheriff Lammars, the FBI would take credit for finding this important evidence. Finger prints lifted from the guns were preserved for a later comparison with possible suspects. The weapon's manufacturing trail as indexed in the FBI's elaborate gun identification archives would reveal the killer's possible Columbian connection.

In that time interval everyone who'd been on the platform when the shooting happened had been moved by Chief Smith into the Clinic building and into its lecture auditorium. Many were nervously smoking cigarettes, an addiction abandoned in the previous four months. All were hysterical, wondering why such a terrible event had happened. They were excitedly talking, comparing what they'd seen to what others had seen. None could forget the shock of seeing the red blood suddenly spurt outward from the neck of General Edison, seeing Madeline Cohen writhing in pain, bleeding profusely as Gus Ginther frantically tried to stop the bleeding, even tearing his white jacket into strips to be used as compresses in the gaping wound.

In the four months these patients had lived at the Owens' Clinic, daily confessing weaknesses to one another, encouraging one another to break individual addictions, on a bi-weekly basis psychoanalyzed by Dr. Gus Ginther, they'd forged strong bonds with each other and with the Clinic's Director.

Dr. Paige was doing his best to insert himself into their highly stimulated conversations. They ignored him. He was not one of them. Several patients recalled seeing him cowardly jump off the platform and hide under it when the shots were first heard. Their only connection to him was that for some reason unknown to them he'd shared a place on the platform on that fateful day.

When Gus Ginther entered the amphitheater, Madelyn Cohen's fresh blood splattered all over his white shirt and trousers, the room became quiet. He calmly sat down on the demonstration table beside the lectern, legs dangling over the table's edge. Everyone turned to face him. They all waited for his analysis of the terrible event that had occurred minutes earlier.

Gus spoke in measured phrases. "At this time, no one knows why this tragedy has happened." His voice cracked. "It's obvious there was some devious motivation behind what occurred out there today."

Pause. A deep silence filled the large classroom.

Finally Gus spoke. "As you've surmised, General Edison died instantly from his wounds. His body has been taken to the morgue at Memorial Hospital."

Another pause.

"The bodies of Madeline, Carlos and Billy Bob have also been taken by ambulance to Memorial hospital." Tears began flowing down Gus's cheeks as he continued, "The Georgia State Medical Examiner is being flown here to analyze their wounds and extract the lethal bullets from their bodies." His voice choking he added, "All died within seconds of their wounds." He was now sobbing as he reached down into his pocket and removed a handkerchief to blot his tears.

There was a deep silence in the room. Several men were also crying as the shock of what had happened began to affect earlier suppressed emotions.

Gus broke the silence. "All of us present on the platform have been ordered by Chief Smith, who in turn was ordered by the regional FBI office in Atlanta to keep all of us sequestered here until released. I've been told by Chief Smith that a team of FBI agents is at this very moment flying by helicopter to take control of the investigation of this tragedy. The FBI will interrogate each of us to establish what we saw, where we were seated the moment the killings happened." Again silence. He added, "We will all be allowed to leave after that. Like you, I'm anxious to go home. Unlike you, I will be traveling home on my bicycle."

Gus looked directly at Henry Paige. "Dr. Paige, Chief Smith has instructed me to tell you that a police car is at the main entrance, waiting to drive you to Memorial Hospital where Madeline Cohen and Carlos Salazar have been taken. As Chief of Staff at Memorial you're needed there. Please go right now."

Paige arose from his seat, happy to get out of this group where he felt unwanted. He hurriedly walked up the steps of the amphitheater, and out the door.

One patient, after scanning the remaining group, asked, "Where's Tom Owens? He was on the platform with us? Why isn't he here?"

Gus replied, "He's in shock and in our first aid room. He believes the bullet that hit the steel microphone stand and deflected into the chest of Carlos was meant to kill him. The FBI, by telephone, has ordered me to keep him in seclusion. They're especially anxious to interview him."

Gus Ginther knew more than he'd just told them. However, as a psychiatrist his ethics meant he would never tell anyone what he'd learned about Tom Owens.

CHAPTER 23
MONDAY AFTER SATURDAY ASSASSINATIONS

As usual, the Clermont Café was closed on Sunday. Monday morning, however, saw it packed with dozens of locals who'd come into town, dozens of tourists from cities and states as far away as Atlanta, Knoxville, Chattanooga, Asheville and Greenville, and dozens of smaller towns and hamlets in between. Television anchormen standing at the foot of the Art Deco sign that read "Clermont Café" were seen recording segments for their evening news telecasts. Newspapers from outside the USA had sent reporters to Clermont for stories. They could be seen in front of the café interviewing all the locals they could find for background material on the previous "Saturday massacre" as they were now calling it.

Everyone wanted to eat in the restaurant where it was widely known that Dr. Paige always ate his meals. The rumor was that on the previous Saturday at the Owens' Clinic he had heroically directed the other two doctors, Ginther and Owens, in their futile attempts to save the lives of the four victims.

Paige was a block away, on his morning "constitutional"

walk from the in town hospital to the Clermont Café for breakfast, when a shout he was coming went up from the crowd outside the restaurant. Instantly klieg lights from TV crews turned the morning dim dawn-light into intense illumination as Paige was videoed walking to the front door. He began to push his way through the crowd waiting for table space within. Tape recorders were crudely pushed into his face. Both newspaper and television reporters yelled questions for his interpretation of the big Saturday event.

"Dr. Paige," shouted the reporter from the *Atlanta Journal*, "Do you believe Saturday's murders were linked to the mafia and their illegal U.S. drug sales?"

"No," he replied, disgust dripping from his single syllable answer.

"Dr. Paige," asked a well known CBS television commentator, "did you know the FBI and the GBI have located the site up on Sugar Loaf Mountain where four snipers fired their deadly bullets?"

"No. I've not heard that. We all know the shots came from the south slope of the mountain. When that damned Addiction Clinic was being constructed I told contractors they were building it in a place susceptible to rock slides and other dangerous catastrophes. But, no one would listen to reason. That mental health facility should have been built as an annex to our in-town hospital."

"Dr. Paige," a local newspaper reporter cried out, "do you believe this tragic event will cause the Owens' Addiction Clinic to close its doors permanently?"

"Let's hope so. Our town doesn't need those drunks and those cocaine addicted outsiders with all their hang-ups coming here."

Having so pontificated, Paige entered the Café for his usual breakfast of two eggs scrambled, hash browns, rye toast with grape jelly, and coffee.

The crowd outside waited and hoped for another celebrity

from the Saturday massacre to appear. Just being outside the local Clermont café gave them a sense of history, a sense of being in the town where the intrigue of the Saturday shooting would be told and retold for generations to come. The rock bluff on top of Sugar Loaf Mountain where the attack took place was easily visible from the street in front of the Café.

Many questions about the Saturday tragic event remained unanswered.

****

Meanwhile, in the isolated region about twenty miles west of Clermont, the area known as Blackberry Mountain Forest Preserve, in a rickety small cabin partially hidden under an overhanging cliff, a cabin beside the small clear stream flowing from a spring deep within the mountain cave, the four assassins were eating a sparse meal of cold pinto beans and yellow kernels of corn from tin cans stocked weeks earlier by Chester Howell.

As the four men were eating the bearded one spoke. "How long we wait in cabin for contact to pick us up? It's been three days since we did what Señor Vanegas sent us to do."

"We wait 'til time right, until search for us stops," said the tall slender Columbian.

"When will time be right? I hate this food. I hate this hideout," said the stout assassin, his ponderous stomach protruding over a trouser belt hanging low on his hips.

"How do we get back to wives in Columbia?" asked the bearded man, his hand shivering from the cold early morning mountain air. "Why can't we build fire in stove so we can get warm?"

"Because," answered the tall slender Columbian, "smoke from chimney would attract military helicopters searching for us." He paused and then added, "Until now you were kept in ignorance about our exit plan. Six days from now in dark, before sun comes up, we take Jeep to bottom of mountain to rendezvous place. We push Jeep into deep place in nearby lake. A panel truck will pick us up, take us short distance to transfer place. In southeastern states Cartel owns vegetable distribution network for delivering South American fruits and vegetables to regional restaurants. Delivery truck has hidden compartment under load of bananas, lettuce, tomatoes and vegetables. We hide inside. Truck will deliver us to Savannah where banana ship will take us to Nassau. From Nassau, Columbian fishing boat takes us to home in Bogotá and our women. Trip will take about three weeks."

The fat Columbian said, "Good."

The stout bearded assassin arose from the crude wooden table where he'd been eating, walked to the cabin door, opened it and threw the empty bean tin can out the door, stood there for a few seconds, expelled a loud stinky flatus, then mused, "Too bad about Carlos. I had son-of-bitch clinic owner in my rifle cross hairs. I don't know why bullet hit Carlos."

"Señor Vanegas will not be happy you missed target," said the tall slender Columbian. "Carlos was son-in-law, father of six of his grandchildren by second mistress. Señor Vanegas hates Tom Owens, blames him for death of oldest daughter of legal wife."

He arose from the table, emitted a loud prolonged belch and then, almost as an after thought said to the stout bearded Columbian, "Señor Vanegas blames Tom Owens for death of oldest daughter of legal wife. He also blames Tom Owens for failure of Clinic to become distribution center for Columbian cocaine. Señor Vanegas will either have you shot, or, he will send you back here to finish what you failed this time...kill Tom Owens."

CHAPTER 24
THIRTEEN MONTHS AFTER CLOSING OF OWENS' CLINIC, OCTOBER 1969

"Gravitas" is defined as "high seriousness, as in a person's bearing, or in the treatment of a subject." The word epitomized Billy Gibson, self-made millionaire, successful building contractor, community mover-and-shaker, and one of the three Clermont County commissioners. Orphaned as a young boy, town drunk by the age of eighteen, saloon brawler, death defying motor cycle racer from age nineteen to twenty-five, no one ever thought young "Billy" would amount to anything.

At age 26 he married a beautiful local Christian girl who saw in him core values of integrity, intelligence and initiative. She reformed him and channeled his potential into becoming a successful entrepreneur who in time cornered the septic tank market in their fast growing rural north Georgia region. Billy Gibson, whose short stocky stature was only five foot six inches, never-the-less walked tall in Clermont County. His serious demeanor and relentless pursuit of worthy goals made him a man to be listened to, a person to be followed. He was determined to succeed at whatever he put his hand and mind to do.

At age fifty-five, his fortune made, as a civic duty to his many friends, neighbors and community admirers, he entered the political arena. He campaigned for county commissioner. As a "local good 'ole boy" he was easily elected. The Gibson lineage traced back to early pioneers in Clermont County. The Gibson family pride was that his great great grandmother on his father's side was a full-blooded Cherokee Indian.

The locals over-whelmingly voted to elect him as one of its three commissioners to govern their County. Once elected his progressive vision began to move the region out of its isolation mentality and into the second half of the twentieth century. This dedication to progress, however, quickly alienated him from most locals with their inbred provincial mind-set.

In Clermont a man with a vision for community growth could be squashed by the locals with their innate fear of strangers. Their resistance to change was maintained by their absolute generational Democratic control of the County Court House. From the sheriff, to the tax collector, to judges, to the recorder of births and deaths, it was all part of a fixed legal system to preserve the status quo.

Reverence for ancestors is interwoven into their unyielding Christian beliefs. Often it's difficult to differentiate one from the other. In the scores of back road county churches it's not uncommon to hear of "preachers" who proudly proclaim, "The King James Bible was good enough for the apostle Paul and therefore good enough for us."

Change was considered disrespectful to pioneer ancestors who'd sacrificed health and often life itself to homestead farms in that early eighteenth century. Those pioneers raised large families, children whose earliest memories were plowing soil embedded with huge rocks, splitting a zillion tree limbs for rail fences, hand milking cows and goats, digging deep wells, shearing wool from sheep, then spinning it into yarn to make cloth for their clothing. Yet in the evening twilight they found time to pick guitar and banjo strings and sing about their simple way of life. It's easy to understand why modern descendants became closely bonded to the land in these hallowed mountains and fertile valleys.

It should be pointed out that they weren't entirely against change. Nearly every house, no matter how humble, had electricity, modern plumbing, television antennas protruding from their roofs, and gasoline powered tractors and hydraulic log-splitters in a backyard shed.

In juxtaposition to their parochialism was the Clermont Chamber of Commerce, mostly composed of generational locals. They encouraged realtors to sell retirement homes to outsiders from Atlanta and other southern metropolitan areas. Prime building sites were located beside the many trout-filled streams, water falls, and mountain tops with a ten mile view. This influx of home buyers "from off" increased the necessity for costly construction of new roads, bridges, extended utilities lines and more schools. Generational "locals" on fixed low incomes were increasingly being forced to sell inherited land once cleared of virgin forests by revered ancestors to pay escalating property taxes to finance all these county improvements. This social dynamic exacerbated already smoldering hostility to rich newcomers building lavish second homes on land once theirs. It was easy for Paige to capitalize on their envy of strangers moving onto their heritage.

Symbolic of this culture clash was the old Memorial Hospital versus the newer but now vacated Owens' Clinic building, a structure which could easily be transformed into a modern hospital. Progressive minded Commissioner Billy Gibson was the spark that ignited this tinder of envy. The controversy over hospitals became an open blaze.

After the Saturday massacre at the Owens' Clinic,

registration for the second group of patients was near zero. Addicts, their senses already fine tuned to the detection of deceit, were wary of coming to a rehabilitation center where assassins might be waiting. They suspected something at the Owens' Clinic was not right. They were correct.

Maintenance salaries, property taxes and utility bills at the now deserted Owens' Clinic went unpaid. Because Tom had refused to permit his clinic from becoming a clandestine distribution center for illegal Columbian drugs, his ex-father-in-law in Bogotá had stopped all funding. Unknown to him, he was again on his ex-father-in-law's list for assassination, since the first attempt failed. No one defies Cartel orders and lives.

After the Owens Clinic finally filled for bankruptcy, Billy Gibson immediately initiated a community campaign to purchase its buildings and ground for the relocation of the old downtown archaic Memorial Hospital to this beautiful spacious forty-acre campus. At a meeting of the County Commissioners his proposal to close memorial Hospital was like a knife plunged into the heart of the "locals." The battle was joined. Billy had the support of those "from off." Paige had the backing of the "locals."

****

The Court House was the official place where political decisions were legalized. However, the Clermont Café was the neutral ground where individual community leaders unofficially met during the restaurant's slow mid-morning hours, the place where the law against closed government meeting ostensibly would not be violated, an impartial place where compromises could be privately negotiated. Billy had requested a mid-morning meeting with Paige at this historic town eatery. His purpose: reach a compromise about their community hospital conflict.

"Shut your damn mouth Billy. You got elected but your

position on the Board of Commissioners is meaningless when it comes to getting things done around here. To get elected you sold your soul to the devil to get campaign money from outsiders. That cursed clinic for drunks and druggies west of town is plagued. No local person is gonna approve buying that doomed site and relocate our hospital out there." Paige leaned back in his chair as he pounded his fist on the table to emphasize his point and also to intimidate his adversary for whom he had contempt, whom he considered intellectually inferior to him. Until that moment Billy Gibson remained relaxed with both arms resting on the table, hands wrapped around a mug of warm coffee. He was not afraid of Paige and his physical threats or his disregard of his intelligence, nor his powerful influence over the "locals." Billy was himself more than a "local." Cherokee blood flowed through his veins.

Paige's belligerent gesture energized Billy who slowly arose to his feet and calmly replied, "Okay, if that's the way you want it, let's go out the back door and into the alley. We'll settle this matter with our fists, privately, just you and me. You ain't man enough to beat me." Billy was now leaning across the table, pointing his stubby calloused fore finger in the face of the town's most beloved doctor. The few mid-morning customers in the café stopped talking, turned to gaze at the confrontation between these two men.

Paige straightened his posture in the chair. "I don't fight stupid people. I out-think 'em." Snarling, leaning forward he added, "...out-thinking you doesn't take much effort."

Billy Gibson again sat down. "I'll use my own money to start a campaign to get public opinion behind me. We're gonna buy that rehab clinic and turn it into a modern hospital. Memorial Hospital's a dinosaur in the field of modern health care. Plaster's falling off the walls. Its halls ain't wide enough for two gurneys to pass one another. It barely meets State hospital standards. It can't be remodeled unless it's completely torn down and rebuilt."

"You're stupid! You're not gonna persuade this community to forsake Memorial Hospital. It's an historical landmark. Besides, you're only one of three commissioners. The other two are in my corner. You're not gonna convince these local folk to relocate it if I don't approve the move, and I don't and I won't."

Gibson countered, "You ain't got the vote of Harold LaQuire. Harold owes me over a hundred thousand dollars for all the septic tanks I buried in his new multimillion dollar golf course community. As the second Commissioner, Harold'll vote with me 'cause a new modern hospital will attract new house buyers into our County, people who will buy all those expensive houses he's building. Don't talk to me about stupid. We all know that for these past years, as Chief-of-Staff, you've been milking your position for all kinds of under-the-table kick-backs. I may lack the education you have, but I ain't stupid. You're as crooked as that old rattlesnake whose head I cut off in my garden yesterday."

When Billy referred to Paige being crooked, the doctor winced, turned to view the few mid-morning patrons sipping coffee to determine if they'd heard Gibson's allegation.

Struggling to keep his voice under control, carefully choosing his words, Paige stammered, "You, you may have new County residents backing you, but, but I have, I have the locals behind me. You haven't seen a fight like it'll be when those locals get riled up. They owe me for saving their lives, owe me for keeping their secrets. I know who has syphilis and gonorrhea and who gave it to them and when they got it. I know whose daughters have had abortions. I know who got them pregnant and when. I know who's gay and who in the gay community has this new mysterious anti-immunology virus and who gave it to them. These people owe me big time, and if I say we don't buy that damn clinic started for drunks, these mountain folk will back me up and vote you out of office next election, vote you out for trying to buy that bankrupt worthless clinic started by that town drunk Tom Owens, a clinic he financed with Columbian Cartel money. This town doesn't need another hospital. The community already has one and it's a damn good one."

At this point Paige, anger flaring, shoved back his chair, stood up and prepared to leave, but not before making a concluding statement. Pointing his recently manicured left index finger at Gibson, he shouted, "You made your reputation installing cement tanks in the ground for people's shit. I made my reputation in this community saving lives and keeping secrets. We'll see who the people support, a shit-hole installer, or a professional health care provider who has for over twenty years saved lives." Paige threw back his shoulders, held his head high as he strutted between empty tables and chairs and hurriedly walked out the front door.

Billy remained seated as he thought, *Septic tanks are better, more modern than that old fashioned three-hole out-house they call Memorial Hospital.* He took a sip from his coffee cup. As he mused about the clash just concluded, he thought, *The real problem here is these old timers don't trust those who've recently moved here. Old timers are afraid of all strangers; afraid somebody's going to take away their past which, they think is their power. I'm more concerned about my children's future than my parents and their parent's past.*

He glanced toward the front door as four tourists entered the restaurant. He thought, *I need to leave and get back to my business.* He dropped two dollars on the table as a tip for Maggie the waitress. He noted Paige had left nothing, not even payment for his cup of coffee. Paige's cheapness sparked another thought in Billy's mind. *I wonder how my great grandfather felt two hundred years ago when his Cherokee wife's relatives were driven off this land and forced to walk 900 miles to Oklahoma in that trail of tears? I wonder how my great grandpa justified the State forcing Cherokees off land they'd occupied for centuries. Many times I've been told that all eighteenth century settlers here in north Georgia paid the government for their homesteads. I wonder if that land-grab state lottery in 1836 by those politicians started all these fearful feelings that someday some stranger is gonna force these locals off their land causing feelings of guilt among us locals. I wonder.*

As he arose to leave he took a final sip of coffee now lukewarm. He thought, *I don't remember much about my father but I do remember him saying, "Fear is the tax conscience pays to guilt." Fear and guilt must be the opposite of trust and a good conscience. Maybe that ought to be my approach to convince voters in Clermont County to buy the Owens' Clinic. Paige may be a skilled doctor, but he's a charlatan who preys on people's fears.*

As Billy walked out the café's front door he stopped, gazed up at the rock cliff at the summit of Sugar Loaf Mountain where the four unknown assassins had perched. While the unsolved mystery of their identity had intensified local feelings of fear for all strangers, this spot had also become a tourist attraction. In the past four months, thousands of strangers had stood here as they gazed up at the top of Sugar Loaf Mountain, the lair of the unknown assassins who'd killed four innocent people on the day of the graduation of the first class of recovering addicts at the Owens' Clinic.

He thought, *This battle over hospitals will be trust versus fear. I'm going to take the high ground of trust in this campaign.* That was his mistake.

****

Eventually the campaign for purchase of the Owens' Clinic to replace the antiquated Memorial Hospital involved everyone. It was impossible to be neutral. The Rotary Club, filled with community leaders, was split between locals and new residents now living in Clermont County. Land developers, mostly locals, were secretly financing Paige's campaign but outwardly wanted a new hospital because health-care was critical to older retired newcomers buying scenic homes within the county. These folk wanted doctors and specialized modern medical equipment nearby for physical emergencies.

Debates were organized by the regional Women's Club. Billy Gibson, though without a college education, won the hearts and minds of all those "from off" because he'd taken the high road of integrity and trust for strangers. Paige was seen by newcomers as being closed minded, prejudiced and self-serving. Many locals with their fear of change were attracted to his biased approach and gave him money to buy newspapers ads and spot commercials on the local 500 watt country music radio station listened to by most locals.

One predictable development was that the campaign quickly became Democrats versus Republicans. The Democratic controlled Court House with its workers along with all their relatives and friends supported Paige. They were the entrenched political "locals."

One dark night Billy Gibson's place of business was spray painted with nasty filthy words that questioned his honesty and genealogy.

All the medical personnel at Memorial Hospital, all "locals," threatened to go on strike if the three Commissioners of Clermont County voted to purchase the Owens' Clinic.

Clermont County was not a peaceful place to live in these months leading up to the big Commissioner's Meeting scheduled for January 8, 1970.

Chapter 25
Thursday Evening, January 8, 1970, Clermont County Court House

The monthly meeting started to get ugly. The three elected officials who were the Clermont County Board of Commissioners had scheduled a vote on whether or not to purchase the now bankrupt Owens' Clinic and make it the new County hospital.

Chairman Ross Jones had just called for the secretary to read the last item on the printed agenda, the item that had drawn approximately three hundred citizens to the meeting to express their opinions. It was the final reading on this controversial issue.

"I move," said Commissioner Billy Gibson, "that Clermont County purchase the now abandoned Owens' Clinic for the sum of three million dollars, the amount of which should be financed by the sale of municipal bonds, and that when this purchase is completed the old Memorial Hospital be closed and the building either sold or torn down."

Chants of, "No! No! No!" arose from a large delegation

within the packed court room now being used for this community issue. Many jumped up from their seats, arms waving, hands clenched into fists.

On the other side of the center aisle another group of citizens began to chant louder, "Yes! Yes! Yes!" Like a cheerleader, a middle aged man wearing a cardigan sweater was standing on the front bench, facing his followers, like a choir director with his hands coordinating their rhythmic chant.

Chairman Ross Jones pounded the oak table with his gavel as he pulled the one microphone on the table close to his mouth. His voice now amplified he shouted, "Silence! Silence! This is a public meeting. I will order this meeting closed if all of you don't sit down and become quiet."

Within the packed court room the crowd's raucous behavior slowly began to wane as each group leader alternating with downward motions of outstretched hands and finger in front of his lips gestured for their followers to sit down and become silent. People on each side of the aisle began sitting down. The chamber again became somewhat quiet.

Chairman Ross Jones, facing the other two Commissioners asked, "Is there a second to this motion?" Without hesitation, Harold LeQuire said, "I second this motion."

Again shouts of, "No. No. No." filled the room. Those on the other side of the center aisle responded by shouting, "Yes. Yes. Yes."

Chairman Jones repeatedly banged his gavel hard on the oak table as he spoke, his mouth again close to the microphone, "Anymore such outbursts and I assure you I will have our Sergeant-at-arms, Deputy Sheriff Hoyt Cross, forcefully usher out of this auditorium, those disrupting this public meeting." He emphasized the word "assure."

Again, moderate silence reigned.

"Now that there has been a second to Commissioner Gibson's motion, I will open this meeting for audience participation. But again let me assure all of you that if there's any more shouting, the leaders of such outbursts will be promptly forced to leave this auditorium. Is that clear? This is America, not Russia. Our laws will be respected, whether or not you agree with them."

A murmur swept across both sides of the crowded assembly.

Chairman Jones reached over and again pulled the one microphone on the Commissioner's table even closer to his mouth. His voice now amplified he calmly instructed, "All who wish to comment about this motion must come forward and speak into that microphone on that chrome post there in the middle of the aisle. Those of you who choose to speak must first state your name and address. It will be recorded by our secretary. Then and only then will I allow your comment to be heard. Your opinion must not be over one minute in duration."

Immediately a long line formed in the middle aisle of the large court house chamber.

One glance at their clothing and it was easy to detect which side of this controversial issue each person represented. For the most part the men who opposed the purchase wore clean blue denim bib overhauls over a faded blue denim shirt, on their feet hunter's boots. Many had beards, some quite long. Most women waiting to express their opposition wore simple gingham dresses, long black and white braided hair hanging down the middle of their back or gathered in buns on top of their heads.

Men who wanted to speak in favor of the motion were also distinguishable by short sleeved open collared colorful sport shirts, designer wrist watches, and Docker slacks. On their feet they wore either leather loafers or hiking shoes. Women waiting to speak in favor of the motion wore preppy L.L. Bean slacks, cardigan sweaters with empty sleeves draped over their shoulders. On their feet they wore sporty bright-hued tennis shoes.

The attire of those in line was a classic display of "locals" versus those "from off."

The lead reporter from the local county newspaper recorded representative comments from both sides of this issue, summarized opinions printed the next day in the *Clermont Clarion*.

"We don't need a new expensive hospital. We have Memorial Hospital. It was good enough for my grandpa and grandma, and it's good enough for me, my wife and my kids."

"The fifty year old Memorial Hospital is a community antique in this twentieth century. Its halls are so narrow it no longer meets today's State standards for hospitals."

"My mother was born and died in that hospital. To tear it down would dishonor her memory."

"Where're the tax payers in this County gonna get three million dollars to pay for that new hospital built for drunks, that place where those four people were murdered? That place has a curse on it."

"Buying the Owens' Clinic which is less than two years old will be the best bargain this county could ever make. The old Memorial Hospital needs to be torn down. Building a new hospital would cost much more than three million dollars."

"We got the best doctor in this world, Doctor Paige, managing Memorial Hospital, and if it's good enough for him, it's good enough for me and my family." What the newspaper didn't say was that this quote was made by the husband of Doctor Paige's nurse, Gretchen. He turned to face Doctor Paige who was quietly seated in the rear of the auditorium. "I say let's give a loud applause for him who's given his life managing our hospital." At the mention of Doctor Paige, those in opposition to buying the Owens' Clinic burst into loud applause.

Finally, to silence the applause, Doctor Paige stood up, his left arm raised high in the air, his first and second fingers forming a "V", his lips forming the words, "Thank you."

Again Chairman Jones gaveled the crowd to silence. "We will now vote on Commissioner Billy Gibson's motion. Those in favor, raise your right hand." Both Billy Gibson and Harold LeQuire promptly raised their right hands.

"Those opposed to this motion raise your right hand." Chairman Jones, smiling at his obvious incongruous statement, raised his hand, then quickly announced, "The motion to purchase the Owens' Clinic is hereby passed by a vote of two for and one against. This meeting is adjourned." He banged his gavel on the oak table. The three Commissioners stood up and quickly exited the room through a back door.

Voices among the opposition to the sale began to shout, "This is not the end of this matter. We'll fight this through the courts and delay this vote until hell freezes over."

Others were yelling, "We'll boycott use of this new hospital until it fails."

****

Fourteen months later, after endless legal battles and court appeals, during which time local attorneys cashed in with large fees, all of which drained the finances of both sides, the matter was finally settled by the courts. The purchase by the Clermont County Commissioners was ruled legal. The formerly bankrupt Owens' Clinic, renamed "The Clermont County Hospital," was refurbished with the necessary modifications that allowed it to pass State standards for rural hospitals. Most of the diagnostic equipment and furniture including beds were moved from the old Memorial Hospital to the new hospital. The old hospital officially closed and its doors padlocked by Sheriff Lammar.

Six months after the commissioner's vote, the new hospital opened for business. However, prolonged litigation had poisoned the minds of a large segment of County citizens. The nursing staff was reduced to only nine because the thirty beds in the new hospital were largely unoccupied. Doctor Paige led a boycott among other Clermont doctors to not send patients to the new hospital, instead using neighboring county hospitals. Diagnostic equipment which required skilled technicians sat unused, their maintenance and salaries a drain on County taxpayers. Only the ER facility in the new hospital was kept busy by indigent patients who paid nothing for hospital services, patients whose medical bills were paid by property tax payers.

At a special election, with 82% of the electorate coming to County polling places, the largest voter turnout in Clermont history, both Billy Gibson and Harold LeQuire, even though "locals," by a close ballot count and recount were voted out of office. Ross Jones was barely re-elected.

The long campaign for the three places on the Board of Commissioners was intense. The community was divided by the bitter rhetoric and lies told by those who had opposed the purchase of the Owens' Clinic. Two local business men, lackey supporters of Doctor Paige, were elected as new Commissioners, thereby assuring that no future motions for change would happen without Paige's approval. This new Board stacked the nine member Hospital Authority Board, (the legal entity which answered only to the County Commissioners), with men loyal to Doctor Page.

The Hospital Authority Board chose, as their first order of business, Dr. Paige as their chairman. He could not undo the purchase of the Owens' Clinic but he now had total control of the new hospital. The former Owens' Clinic became the official Clermont County hospital.

But Dr. Paige now had a new vision: Use this former Owens' Clinic only as a temporary facility until a new taxpayer financed much larger hospital could be constructed on the site of the old Memorial Hospital on downtown Main Street and name it Paige Memorial Hospital. It would be his final legacy for his life of service to "his" community.

Billy Gibson had taken the high road in his re-election campaign. He emphasized trust and change for a growing County. Even though a "local," he'd lost his bid for re-election because the majority of the old timers didn't trust him because he proposed too many changes within the County. One proposed change that tipped the vote against him was his proposed new zoning ordinance that would make it illegal to have even one rusty junk abandoned automobile in the yard of any house, whether owned or rented. The fine for not obeying was $100 plus cost of towing by the County if the owner refused to remove it.

The fact that the Owens' Clinic had been purchased and was now the new county hospital was a hollow victory for Billy Gibson.

****

The conflict about hospitals in Clermont County was never the new Owens' Clinic versus the old Memorial Hospital. The real issue was within the souls of the "locals" and their unacknowledged deeply embedded fear and resentment of all "strangers" moving into Clermont County. This fear and resentment would soon erupt into a series of heinous crimes.

CHAPTER 26
MONDAY, MAY 17, 1971

"Come in, Mrs. Gist. Please take a seat." Peggy Gist entered the psychiatrist's office, cautiously sat down in one of two brown leather cushioned chairs. Doctor Ginther closed the door and sat down in the chair opposite hers. She straightened her dress as she crossed her legs, right over left, then left over right. Her left foot was nervously jiggling. She was not conscious of this outward display of her inner feelings, body language, however, duly noted by her therapist.

"Since opening my counseling practice here in Clermont this past week, you're my first patient."

"I'm honored." She smiled. His honest admission of vulnerability inclined her to trust him. Perhaps he wasn't like other men in her life. "My husband and I have admired your work. As the Director of the Owens' Clinic you were so successful in curing people of their addictions. What a shame it ended as it did, with those four gruesome murders."

"Forgive me when I correct what you've just said. Addicts never overcome their chemical dependency, are never cured. They just learn its cause, learn to change their lifestyle, avoid tempting social situations, and are constantly strengthening their mental defenses and moral resolve. In the realm of addiction therapy we say an addict is always recovering. Recovery is an on-going life-long process."

"Whatever. I'd call what you just stated a permanent cure." She didn't like being corrected. Ginther made a mental note of her intransigent attitude. She slightly raised her head back, her nose pointing up, as she replied, "Well, it's a shame the Owens' Clinic was forced to file for bankruptcy and the assassins who caused it never captured."

"Yes, as you say." He purposely agreed with her so as not to build a barrier about the real reason why she'd come to him. He added, "It's my gut feeling the assassins fled these mountains within weeks after killing those four people. They were professionals and no doubt had an elaborate escape plan." His mind morphed into the bitter memory of that dreadful day months earlier. Yet fresh in his mind was his shattered dream for restoring chemically addicted people to a normal life of sobriety.

"A few months after that Saturday blood bath my husband was contacted by twenty of the survivors. They wanted to hire him to sue you as the Director of the Clinic, and against Tom Owens as its owner."

"So I heard." Gus smiled as he responded with an old cliché, "No one can get blood out of a turnip." He added, "The sparse assets of the Clinic were frozen by the court during the many legal appeals. Neither Tom nor I had any wealth. The County's subsequent purchase of its vacant facilities and replacing the antiquated downtown Memorial Hospital with it was finally achieved. Paige is now leading a movement to boycott it."

Gus, perceiving her uneasiness, realizing she didn't want to talk further about a defunct hospital, asked, "Why did you want to talk to me today?"

Peggy readjusted herself in the leather-cushioned chair. Her mind was burdened, troubled with personal problems. Slowly she began to speak, her soft voice in despondent tones, glazed eyes staring down at the carpeted floor. "You just mentioned Doctor Paige." Glancing up, she gave her therapist a squinting sideways glance, then again lowered her gaze. "He's the reason I've come to you today. Last year I didn't want to go to him for medical relief but with the unexpected overseas death of my parents, circumstances were such that I had no choice. After laboratory tests he informed me I'm in the early secondary stage of syphilis." She looked up, stared directly at her psychologist as she gauged his reaction to what most people would consider an alarming disclosure.

During his psychiatric internship Gus learned that nothing a patient says should startle a therapist. His countenance remained stoic. Peggy was pleased. She interpreted this dispassionate reaction as non-judgmental of her sexual disease.

"You're saying Paige has confirmed his diagnosis with the necessary blood tests?"

"He tells me he has, including a spinal tap done down at Emory Hospital."

"How has he been treating your condition?" He avoided using the word syphilis.

"I'm given weekly antibiotic injections by Dr. Paige himself, in private. The injections are painful and expensive, but they're curing me. All of my symptoms are disappearing. I no longer have vaginal sores, a skin rash, or frequent headaches."

Ginther leaned back in his chair as he recalled what he'd learned in medical school about this dreaded infectious disease. He said, "One hundred years ago a diagnosis of syphilis was tantamount to death but not so today. Syphilis is caused by the bacterium treponema palladium which in its early two stages responds well to antibiotics." He emphasized "early stages." "Since Paige has been treating you with antibiotics you should be in remission if treatment was started before the third and last stage of the disease."

"Doctor Paige assures me his treatment is curing me."

"Before treatment is started, it's important to know which one of its three stages the disease is in. I'm certain Doctor Paige determined when you first contacted the disease." It was a question, not a statement of fact. He needed to know for certain.

"He has. Many years ago, before I moved here to Clermont, I had an affair with a Baltimore man who infected me. About a year later the first symptoms appeared, sores within my vagina. Back then I didn't know what caused them. The sores healed without treatment and disappeared. I figured they weren't serious. Now fourteen years later they've reappeared. Doctor Paige's diagnosis is that my disease is in its early secondary stage."

"Well, from what you've told me, it appears you're fortunate to have been properly treated by a good doctor and your disease is now being cured." Gus made eye contact with her as he further inquired, "But that's not the real reason why've you come to me. Is there another problem related to your recovery?"

Tears welled up in her eyes as she again lowered her head. "From the beginning my husband and I have had what we call an open marriage. In the early days of our marriage we enjoyed a physical relationship with one another. However, as our marriage accumulated years our sexual urges have expanded into different realms. For many years Charlie's been having affairs with women he visits on a regular basis in Atlanta. He's also had many sexual dalliances with divorced women here in north Georgia. I don't know how many or whom he visits. He plays the field. With all his money and power it's not difficult for him to find vulnerable women."

Gus was repulsed by what he was hearing but didn't dare allow his revulsion to be apparent to his patient. He responded by saying, "And you and Charlie previously agreed to this deviation from your marriage vows."

"No. Our marriage vows excluded sexual fidelity. We wrote

our own vows which were spoken before our local probate judge. On the day we were married we agreed our relationship would be more of a contract for social respectability, not an inhibitor of intimate personal preferences. I agreed not to inhibit Charlie's strong sexual desires."

Gus did something no practicing therapist should do. He expressed an assumption about his patient. "Now Charlie wants a divorce because he's learned you have a serious highly infectious disease?"

"Yes and no." With both hands she began rubbing the back of her neck, her head lowered, her chin on her chest, eyes tightly closed. "Yes, he wants a divorce, and no he doesn't know I had syphilis and have possibly infected him."

Gus waited several seconds before asking, "Do you want a divorce?"

"I don't know. Not because I had syphilis or because I've infected him and he likely now has it."

Ginther noted she'd used the past tense when referring to her disease. He asked, "Then why?"

"My husband is prone to violence. I'm afraid he might kill me."

Their conversation lapsed into silence. Gus was wondering if Paige had reported this case of syphilis to the National Center for Disease Control and Prevention (NCDC) in Atlanta. Gus again asked, "You said your husband doesn't know you had syphilis?"

"Yes." The fact he now used the past tense gave her a renewed sense of hope.

"It's highly likely he also has the disease. In years past you've infected him just as your Baltimore philanderer infected you. It's likely your husband has infected many women in Atlanta and also here in Clermont County. It's possible he will re-infect you."

Peggy Gist made eye contact with her therapist who knew she was about to reveal a long hidden secret in her life. She hesitated, crossed her legs, smoothed out her dress before saying, "I've not been the traditional wife to Charlie. In the past twenty years we've both had sexual relationships outside of our marriage. At times I'm heterosexual when Charlie and I have enjoyed a physical relationship. However, at other times, I'm also inclined to want sexual experiences with women." She paused, uncrossed her legs, gazed up into Gus's stoic face. This was a second revelation she thought might sidetrack her therapist from the real reason she'd come to him for help. She was testing his skills as a therapist. She waited for him to respond.

He said, "I've suspected your androgynous orientation."

A puzzled look on her face she asked, "What caused you to suspect my lesbian preference?"

"There's no definitive profile, just clues. You fit the broad general profile: etiology, personality, appearance, behavior, dysfunctional home in your early years."

"My sexual orientation in this backward mountain culture would black list me from all community activities. I've tried to keep it a secret, except for the local women I've loved, women who know how to keep secret such intimate relationships."

There was a lull in their conversation. Finally Gus said, "Back to this disease, syphilis, you have, or had. I don't know why Dr. Paige has not reported it to the State Health Department, as the law requires. Such contagious diseases can destroy a community. Therefore the law says the State Health department must be informed. Under penalty of jail confinement the primary infected person must reveal the names of all individuals with whom they've had sexual relations within the past three years. Because the prime infected person can't remember everyone, all regional newspapers publish announcements seeking people who have had a sexual experience with the prime person. All who come forward are tested for the disease. If they test positive then the detectives will broaden their search for other possible infected people. This investigation goes on until everyone they check is tested negative for syphilis."

Shocked by this revelation, Peggy responded, "State health detectives investigate every person who's had even one sexual contact with an infected person?"

"Yes. The law is strictly enforced. A physician will lose his license if within thirty days he fails to report an infected person."

"My husband would be afraid such a disclosure would destroy his law practice. For the past few years he's been pursuing a billion dollar class action lawsuit against a mega-insurance corporation. He's already won in the lower courts. If he wins again in the Federal Court of Appeals, and the odds of winning are good, his fee will be over eight hundred million dollars. If his clients learn he has syphilis, they'd likely transfer the litigation to another law firm and he'd lose that high fee."

"Wow! Eight hundred million is a lot of money to lose. That's a powerful motivation to kill!" A chill swept over Ginther's body as he realized his duty to report this case of a highly infectious disease to State authorities, and the possible violent response of his patient's husband.

"That, however, is not why I wanted to talk to you."

"Then what's the problem?" Gus leaned back, afraid of what he might hear next.

"In my mind I'm beginning to hear voices, voices telling me to kill Dr. Paige, kill him for reasons I don't understand. These voices in my mind are getting louder and louder. I hate men." She paused as if hearing what she'd just vocalized was an emotional relief. For the first time she'd openly expressed this long-suppressed strong impulse.

"Have these voices ever told you to take your own life?"

"Yes. When Doctor Paige first told me I had syphilis, I left home and drove down to Atlanta where I got a motel suite. For several days I drank whiskey and stayed drunk. In my intoxicated stupor I felt I didn't want to live any longer. In the middle of the night I purposely overdosed on sleeping pills. The hotel housekeeper found me early the next morning when she came in to make the bed. The manager phoned for an ambulance. The ER staff at the Fulton County Hospital pumped my stomach. My husband doesn't know I tried to kill myself."

"You said you hate men. What kind of relationship did you have with your father? What was your father's relationship with your mother?"

"My father was the only heir to his great grandfather's business of manufacturing guns, both rifles and hand guns. He traveled continuously to sell weapons to foreign nations. He was seldom home. When home he never showed me any affection. The only attention he gave me was to teach me how to become an expert marksman with rifles and handguns. Also, my father was a womanizer. And my mother was into one sexual affair after another. Our house on Chesapeake Bay was like a brothel. I left home after one of my mother's house guests raped me. I was eighteen. I fled to Baltimore and there had an affair with a crooked attorney, a State senator. I lived with him for two months. He knew he had syphilis and for some insane reason deliberately transmitted it to me. In the past ten years I've not returned home. I did write my mother once, shortly after I left home and told her where I was living but told her never to contact me. They didn't. They never really cared where I was. Apparently, however, my mother told my nanny where I was, the nanny who raised me. When my parents were killed in that airplane crash in France, it was my nanny who told Maryland authorities I'd married, changed my last name, and was living here in Clermont."

"You hate all men because of your father's lack of love for you?"

"Could that be true?"

"Perhaps. But why do you have these feelings of wanting to kill Dr. Paige?"

"I have good reason to believe he's having an affair with Gretchen, his nurse."

"Really? But that's not a reason to kill him."

"Yesterday I went to his office for my regular injection. For privacy's sake, I always enter by the back door. It's usually locked. Gretchen comes and unlocks it. This time, however, the door wasn't locked. As I entered, in a closet down the hall, I caught a glimpse of Dr. Paige and Gretchen in a very close embrace. They never saw me. As I passed by Gretchen's receptionist desk I saw my chart lying open, my chart describing my disease." She emphasized the words "my" and "open."

She gave Ginther a hard stare to make certain he caught those words. She continued, "If Gretchen knows I'm being treated for syphilis, the entire town will soon know. Can you imagine what such a story would do to my social life, to my status in this community?" She politely blew her nose on a tissue.

"So, you think Paige has violated the doctor-patient confidential relationship? You think Gretchen knows you have syphilis and might tell others?"

"I know she will. Paige is like my philandering father, like my mother's house guest who raped me, like my Baltimore lover who intentionally gave me syphilis, like my husband who now wants a divorce because I deny him sexual intercourse." She paused and then concluded, "I hate all men. Their minds are always focused on sex. They don't understand that a woman wants more than a sexual relationship." Again she blew her runny nose, this time forcefully.

"And you believe that's the reason why you hate all men?"

"Men don't care who I really am. They only see me as a female, a woman with a body which arouses them sexually.

They never see me as a person. All they want from me is sex to relieve their testosterone buildup." She lowered her gaze and her voice as she concluded, "It's the curse of being a beautiful woman."

"You have the problem all beautiful women have. Marilyn Monroe had it. It appears that was the reason in August of '62 she killed herself at age 37. Most men can't get pass their lust for a beautiful female body. They can't see her as a human who primarily wants spiritual affection, the sexual intimacy a secondary sealing of true love."

There was another pause in their conversation. She gave a deep sigh. Her voice almost a whisper, she said, "In the past few weeks these voices within my head are getting louder and louder."

"What are these voices telling you?"

"They're telling me to kill Doctor Paige, kill Gretchen." She was nervously gripping her moist hands together, face scowling, pupils of her eyes enlarged, her stare non-focused.

Gus arose from his chair. He walked over and sat down in the chair behind his desk, for several minutes meditating, silently reviewing her symptoms and responses to his questions, his hands steepled beneath his chin. Several times he swiveled back and forth in his desk chair as Peggy Gist watched, anticipating his diagnosis of her state of mind.

Finally he said, "I'm going to refer you to a medical specialist at Emory University Hospital in Atlanta, an immunopathologist, for a second opinion about the correctness of Dr. Paige's diagnosis of syphilis in the early secondary stage. I don't know why he's not reported your disease to the State authorities. I want to be certain you have syphilis and, if true, what stage you're in. He reached for a book on his desk top, a listing of all Georgia medical specialists. "I'll arrange an emergency appointment for you. When I receive that second medical opinion, we'll talk again."

He didn't tell her, but he was concerned about three

possibilities. One, since both husband and wife were having extramarital affairs, some local, others in Atlanta, both were at a greatly increased risk for contacting a mysterious newly discovered virus that attacks the body's immune system, especially those who have syphilis. Two, the injections given her by Paige require special equipment and special training. He wasn't sure Paige had such skills or equipment. Three, her references to hearing voices within her head, voices that might be the forerunner to the last stage of syphilis, the stage known as neurosyphilis, the stage where irreversible damage is done in the central nervous system, especially to the part of the brain where fantasy begins to trump reality.

Making direct eye contact, he said, "Tell me more about the voices you're hearing."

CHAPTER 27
TUESDAY, MID-MORNING,
JUNE 1, 1971

Just prior to Peggy Gist's second therapy session, two weeks after Dr. Ginther had sent her to Atlanta for extensive tests by an immunopathologist, the detailed in-depth reports arrived back on his desk. It was a "Jane Doe" report, no actual patient name given, only the attending physician, Ginther, knowing the patient's identity.

It was Monday morning, shortly after nine o'clock. Just as Gus entered his office a postman with a registered certified Postal delivery package arrived. After signing for it, and a show conversation to the delivery person, Gus sat down in his desk chair, cautiously opened the bulky envelope. As he scanned its contents, he immediately knew Peggy Gist's disease was in its third terminal stage.

He noted all the graphs about blood chemistry, spinal taps, MRI brain scans, and serology tests. The conclusion: she was in the third stage of syphilis, the stage, strangely enough, where the patient has no more visible symptoms. Paige had incorrectly diagnosed her disease! He'd said she was in the early secondary not in the late tertiary stage. Sixteen years earlier, after the disease's inception, the bacteria had slowly progressed into its final phase known as neurosyphilis, an irreversible non-curable infection of the central nervous system. In this terminal stage the patient suffers from a slow invasion by the *Treponema pallidum* bacterium into nerves controlling some specific body organ.

According to the Emory report the syphilis bacterium had settled within the precise region of the brain where, under normal healthy conditions, reality dominates fantasy and core beliefs control behavior. In her case the pathogens were short circuiting these micro-electrical brain synapses and reversing them.

After a thorough study of the report, Gus began to mentally prepare himself for how he could compassionately reveal this grievous information to his patient. He immediately decided her husband should be present when he told her of her terminal illness. There was the statistical probability he also had the disease because of sexual contacts with his wife. Having him present at this critical moment in their marriage seemed to be the right thing to do.

He was especially concerned about the "voices" she claimed to be hearing. These "voices" could induce violent behavior. He knew that as her disease progressed she'd be more inclined to act out their commands. He was concerned about her statement that she hated all men, especially Paige.

He finally decided to wait until tomorrow to meet with them. A one day delay would give him time to formulate a strategy about how to inform her she was in the incurable last stage, and that her husband probably also had the same disease.

Late Monday afternoon Gus telephoned Peggy Gist and set an urgent appointment for her and her husband the following morning, Tuesday, 10 o'clock.

****

"Come in, Mr. and Mrs. Gist. Please take a seat." He closed the office door, walked over to his desk, sat down in his chair across from the two who now faced him. "Peggy, I'm sure you know the reason for this visit. The Atlanta lab has sent me their written analysis of the extensive tests you took down there nearly two weeks ago." He opened her file folder lying on his desk, lifted out the bulky report.

"Well," she said, apprehension almost overcoming her, "What does the report say?" She reached into her purse for a tissue, dabbed her nose with it, tightly gripping it in her right hand. Her left hand was shaking as she anticipated what she'd hear. Her attorney husband, hands steepled just below his chin, was at the same time alternately glancing over at his wife then back at Ginther, his facial expression questioning what would happen next.

"Charles, has Peggy told you the reason for this visit to my office today?"

"Partially." He gave her another long perplexed look, as he continued, "Apparently it has something to do with her health."

Gus replied, "This visit has everything to do with your wife's health, which I'm sure is important to you as her husband, but also important to you because you too are likely infected with the same disease that may soon take her life."

"Take my life?" She stood up as she asked, "Is that what you just said?"

"Yes. There's no easy way to tell you what must be said. According to this report you have perhaps six months yet to live. With treatment, this time might be lengthened." He quickly arose, walked around the desk to stand beside her as he'd noted her face had become pale as if she was close to fainting. He eased her back down into the cushioned chair. "I wish there was some other way to tell you this bad news, but I must inform you that your disease is in its final incurable phase."

167

With Peggy now seated, Gus walked back around his desk, sat down, all the while keeping his eyes fixed on both her and her husband. Looking first at one, then at the other, his words were deliberate. "It's likely that between the two of you and your dissimilar sexual orientations, you've infected dozens of others. And those you have infected have in turn also infected others. It's likely there are several hundred people who now have syphilis because of your sexual proclivities." He paused and then added, "According to Georgia Law I must report your case of syphilis to the State Health authorities. Under penalty of severe fines and prison terms, you will be forced to identify as best you can everyone with whom you've had a sexual relationship within the past two years. Government health detectives are mandated to begin the extensive process of tracing the disease back to all those with whom you've had intimate contact, and then tracing those with whom they've had sexual contacts. It's a long extensive investigative procedure to prevent this deadly disease from becoming epidemic."

Charles Gist jumped up from his chair. "You can't do that! Such knowledge among my many clients will destroy me, destroy my law practice." He didn't say it, but he feared his clients in the pending billion dollar lawsuit would transfer the case to another law firm and he'd lose most, if not all, of his multimillion dollar fee.

Leaning forward in his desk chair, Gus replied, "I'm sorry but it's the law. I could lose my license if I don't comply within thirty days after I learn of this disease in a patient. I'll be filing my report to State health authorities this coming week, probably Friday."

"Ginther, you son-of-a bitch!" Charles Gist walked over behind Ginther's desk, leaned over, his face just inches in front of his face, spit out the words, "Why haven't I been told earlier about this? Now I find out exactly what her disease is, syphilis. That means she…," and he pointed to his weeping wife, "…has infected me."

"That's correct. There's a ninety percent probability that lab tests will show you also have syphilis. However, if tests show you have it, it will be in the early curable stage." As Gus stood up, Charles Gist backed away as he observed the doctor's clenched right fist. "Ginther, how much money do I need to pay you to delay filing that report for at least six months? For starters, I'll pay fifty thousand dollars." Charles quickly ran the fingers of his right hand through his bushy head of graying hair.

Gus's eyes were squinting as he stared directly into Charles Gist's face, "My ethics are not for sale."

"I'll pay you one hundred thousand dollars right now, today, if you'll delay your report for six months." Again, the quick fingers through his head of thick hair.

"You can't buy me. I'm not for sale."

After several seconds of failing to stare down this doctor, Charles Gist turned to face his wife, "Sixteen years ago when you married me you knew you had syphilis. Why didn't you tell me? Then you could have been cured, you could have…."

"Back then I didn't know I had syphilis."

"You were sleeping around," he accusingly sneered.

"So were you," she quickly retaliated.

Charlie began to stutter, his normally logical mind checkmated by her retort. "You, you knew, you… you…."

Gus interrupted him, "For some reason which I can't understand she was deceived by Doctor Paige who misdiagnosed her disease. In a previous therapy session she told me you two have had what you call an open marriage where you both have been sexually permissive, you with women and she with women." He gave this menacing attorney a stern look. "Your anger is misdirected. I'm only the messenger bringing to both of you the bad news, for which I'm deeply sorry." He added, "I don't know why Paige hasn't already reported you to the Georgia State health authorities."

"I'm going to sue both you and Paige. I'll destroy you both as physicians, ruin you as a psychiatrist." He made a threatening move toward Gus who stood his ground.

In Gus's mind he thought about how this conference wasn't proceeding as he'd hoped. Charles Gist's violent temper, which his wife had referred to in her first session, was now confirmed in his mind. This man in his present agitated state-of-mind was potentially capable of murder. The probable loss of his eight hundred million dollar fee in his class-action law suit was obsessively uppermost in his mind. Gus instantly concluded Charles Gist was a man without moral restraints.

The tone of Gus's voice changed. His words became dispassionate, composed, carefully chosen. Without backing away he responded, "Your wife has a terminal disease. You also may be infected. If you begin treatment at once, you can be cured, but your wife's life expectancy is terminal, at best one year. It's a slow moving disease. I'm sorry I had to be the doctor to give you this bad news."

Charles Gist again stepped closer to the doctor, fists clenched, his face inches from Ginther's. This time Gus backed away. Neither was aware that Peggy was extracting from her purse a gun. She stood up, shouted, "Shut up, both of you!" She pointed the pistol at her husband, then at Gus. Both turned to face her, both frightened and afraid of what she might do next. Slowly Gus began to separate himself from Charles, inching over to stand behind his desk. Quietly he said, "Peggy, put the gun down."

She lowered the weapon, then collapsed into the chair, sobbing, "Why didn't Doctor Paige tell me two years ago?"

Gus stepped over to her, put his arm about her shoulder as he carefully extracted the gun from her collapsed hand, laid it on his desk. "Peggy, don't give up. There's always new drugs, new medicines being developed." There was no conviction in his voice.

"Did you say my mind will experience delusions? Are you saying those voices I've been hearing will grow louder, and I won't even be aware of this behavior change?"

"Yes."

Attorney Gist, his rage inflamed, quickly stepped over to strike her. His intent was thwarted as Gus slid his hand across the desk, picked up the gun, pointed it at him.

"If you hit her, I'll be forced to shoot you in the leg."

"Ginther, if you report our disease to the CDC I'll kill you. Your report will cost me the biggest fee in my legal career. If you report that my wife and I have this disease you'd better keep looking over your shoulder because I'm gonna have my revenge, and soon." Gist, his anger somewhat abated, moved across the room, headed for the door.

"My report will be sent to the Center for Disease Control on Friday."

"You're a dead man, Ginther!" Charles Gist walked out the office door and hurriedly began walking down the hall toward the building's outer door.

Gus followed him out into the hall shouting after him, "You should be angry at Paige, not me. He's been incorrectly doctoring your wife's disease."

Charles Gist didn't hear him.

In that moment, alone in Ginther's office, the voice inside Peggy's head told her to pick up both her gun and her file from the desk of her therapist. She quickly stuffed them into her large purse and walked out of his office. Gus, still standing out in the hall by the entrance to his counseling suite, met her, tried to persuade her to return for more therapy.

"I must go. My husband's driving. I need to ride with him back home." She left.

Once inside their auto Charles informed his wife that on

the previous day Paige had urgently requested that he come to his office to receive some important information.

"Before driving back to our house, I need to stop and see what that son-of-a bitch wants. You can wait here in the car. I won't be long." After Ginther's revelation about his wife's disease, Charles assumed he knew why Paige wanted to talk. He was partly right and partly wrong in this assumption.

The following day, June 2, Clermont, a small mountain city in north Georgia would become the news center of the nation... again.

CHAPTER 28
MONDAY NOON, JUNE 1, 1971

"You want what?" Charles Gist jumped up from his chair when he heard what Paige had just said. Attorneys are always supposed to know the answer before they ask a question. This, however, was a startling demand by the man in the white coat, the man seated behind the walnut desk in his clinic's office, stethoscope dangling around his neck, the power figure in this encounter between two respected citizens in Clermont County.

"You heard me," replied Doctor Henry Bartram Paige, town icon of respectability, custodian of the health of Clermont County citizens. "I expect you to purchase my house on the shore of Lake Nelson for ten million dollars." He paused as he gave his opponent a twisted sneering smile. "My house out on Lake Nelson is valued at least one hundred thousand dollars. However, as we both know, value is in the mind of the buyer. I'm offering it to you for only ten million." He was obviously enjoying the moment, savoring the sweet revenge for which he'd waited eleven years.

Attorney Gist sat down, sensing more information was about to be given him by this adversary. "Why should I buy your damn lake house?" The fingers of his right hand reflexively raked his head of thick hair, followed by a second quick pass through.

"From rumors I hear over at the Court House, you're about to win a two billion dollar class-action lawsuit against an international insurance company. It's easy to estimate your fee, a sum I figure will be about eight hundred million." He was looking directly into the face of the man seated in the chair across from his desk. "I congratulate you on this professional victory." A fleeting smile quickly disappeared as he leaned forward, his voice snarling. "I remember when you stole five hundred thousand from me in that lawsuit against me and the hospital, that lawsuit which nearly ruined me financially. Now it's my turn to share in your wealth, wealth you won't even miss when you get that check from the Empire Insurance Corporation."

Sensing Paige had more to say, Charles Gist leaned back in the maroon leather-upholstered chair while looking directly into Paige's face. From the inside of his suit coat pocket he took out a large black cigar, pulled off the cellophane wrapper, threw it into the wastebasket at the end of Paige's desk, bit off the cigar's end, spit it out and onto the well worn frayed carpeted floor, placed it into his mouth. From his left coat pocket he took out a wooden match. With a sweeping movement scratched its tip on the bottom of the walnut chair in which he was sitting. As the match ignited, its flame poised at the end of his cigar, Charles still staring directly into Paige's eyes said, "Mind if I smoke?"

Without waiting for an answer he touched the flame to the tobacco's tip, inhaled deeply, blew smoke in Paige's direction and then replied, "Why should I pay you ten million dollars?" His voice was calm but dripping with sarcastic overtones.

"Because if you don't I'll release certain damaging information into our community, information I possess, information that will destroy you, destroy your law practice, destroy your reputation, and," Paige paused for effect, "...and destroy your lawsuit."

"And what possible information do you have that could destroy me?" With his right hand Gist removed the cigar from his mouth, blew a cloud of bluish-white smoke up toward the ceiling as with his little finger he tapped the end of the cigar, thus dropping ash onto the carpeted floor of Paige's office.

Paige replied, "Information that both you and your wife are carrying the dreaded disease of syphilis..." and his voice grew louder, "...and you have already infected scores of the good innocent citizens in our lovely mountain community, information State health detectives will soon be extracting from you, identification of each woman with whom you've slept in the past five years, every woman who's had an secret affair with your lesbian wife. There will be newspaper bulletins and radio blurbs asking women you've forgotten, women you didn't remember, women your wife infected, all to come forward, be identified so they might be tested for the dreaded disease. They'll be given a blood test to determine if they also have syphilis as you do." Paige added, "You'll be ruined."

For perhaps a minute there was a profound silence between them before Paige again spoke. His voice grew louder but slower as he pointed his index finger at the man seated across from his desk. "You're a profligate sex addict. Your wife is a discreet but adventurous lesbian. This truth made public about you both and your disease would throw this community into a panic. Both of you will be shunned. Public awareness about your disease will cause you to lose your law practice, cause you to lose your eight hundred million dollar fee from the Empire Insurance Corporation." Paige knew he had the winning hand in this contest of mental poker.

With a sneer on his face Paige finally added, "Those people you and your wife have infected will sue you and take what remains of your wealth. You'll be ruined!" This was the moment for which he waited for over a decade!

Charles Gist gagged. Paige's recitation of public responses to their disease caused him to suddenly inhale smoke from his cigar. His voice choking, his demeanor bluffing, he replied, "What'd you say? Syphilis? Can't be." However, his session with Dr. Ginther earlier this day was still fresh in his mind. He also was aware that for the past several years he'd been unable to have a sexual relation with his wife because of her spasmodic occurring vaginal sores. He'd compensated by having affairs too numerous to count with Atlanta women, with divorcees and widows within Clermont County.

Charles Gist knew a "trump hand" when he saw one.

Henry Paige also knew he had a winning hand. His voice was now soft and low as he repeated, "Ten million is all I expect from you for the purchase of my lake house." His voice now lowered even more, he coldly added, "You know God made only so much water-front land. You'll be buying one of the most desirable houses on Lake Nelson." He smiled the smile of a victor.

"You're bluffing," Charles shouted and then added, "There's such a thing as doctor-patient confidentiality. You can't violate that ethical code without losing your credibility in this community and a probable law suit from me." He nervously took a long drag on his cigar, this time blowing the smoke off to one side and up into the air, away from his adversary.

"You're a professional attorney. You possess the same client confidentiality privilege as I do. We both know there are a dozen ways to leak information and not violate our code of ethics."

"What if my wife has some other disease, a non-infectious disease like vaginal warts which is what she told me she has?" Paige saw him swallow and knew he was lying.

Paige now played his trump card. "Lab tests don't lie." He

laid his hand on an impressive folder on his desk. "All tests done in Atlanta confirm she has syphilis. I'm legally bound to report all infectious diseases to the Atlanta Center for Disease Control. I haven't reported your infectious disease earlier because I had no proof. It's most likely you also have syphilis. I'll delay reporting both of you until after you receive your check for eight hundred million and I receive my cashier's check for ten million. After you've received your attorney's fee you'll be fabulously rich. In this community at that time the news you and your wife both have syphilis won't make any difference to you. With your remaining multimillion you can both move to Europe, hire the best European doctors who will begin treatment for the cures to your diseases. And then you can live happily ever after, somewhere in Europe."

"You son-of-a-bitch!"

Paige got up from his desk chair, matter-of-factly walked over to the office door, opened it as he said, "I'll begin getting the papers ready for the sale of my lake house."

Seemingly defeated, Charles Gist arose from his chair, shoulders slumped, cigar clenched tightly between his fingers as he moved slowly toward the open office door. His thinking process had been check-mated.

Paige, as a parting twist of the verbal knife in his enemy's heart, calmly said, "After we both get our checks, as a good will gesture, I'll include in the sale price all the lavish furnishings at my lake house, even my fishing boat." In his mind he was thinking, *revenge, how sweet it is.*

Paige was correct about the sweetness of revenge, but such sweetness is brief. Revenge is like a boomerang. For a short distance it flies in the direction hurled, but always returns to the one who hurled it and may strike and injure the hurler. Vengeance is the prerogative of God, not man. Revenge, the antithesis of forgiveness, was to cause the inevitable doom of Henry Paige.

CHAPTER 29
EARLY WEDNESDAY MORNING, JUNE 2, 1971

Several months before the County purchased his Clinic, Tom's extreme jaundiced condition foreshadowed an early death. Wisely he'd had the title of everything he owned, which wasn't much but included the forty acre defunct Clinic, transferred to his wife. Part of Vera's final sale settlement with Clermont County Commissioners was that she be given a life-time lease on the house located on one-half acre on the north side of the forty acres of his now defunct Clinic. Money paid by the County for the clinic's purchase was reduced by about fifty percent because of large attorney fees, extensive court costs, liens, unpaid back property taxes, employee's severance wages and personal income taxes. But it was enough to provide Vera a comfortable income for the remainder of her life.

Since the hospital's purchase of the Owens' Clinic a year earlier, inadequate County funding had allowed the once beautiful landscaped grounds to become filled with weeds. Only about six acres adjacent to the newly refurbished main building were being maintained. In the year since the county's acquisition of the property, the "Billy Gibson's folly," as its detractors were calling it, was near to closure. The secret strategy by the revengeful Doctor Paige and his physician cronies to send their sick patients to neighboring county hospitals reduced income at the Clermont hospital to near zero. Each month County Commissioners had to subsidize the new health facility with over fifty thousand dollars, a heavy drain on meager County resources. The occupancy rate of the thirty-bed hospital averaged less than three patients per week and these were mostly indigent Hispanics whose care was paid by precious tax dollars. It was a very low point in the conflict over hospitals in Clermont County.

Tom Owens had again become a recluse. He and wife Vera lived a simple lifestyle. His new faith in a "Higher Power" had evaporated as he slipped into deeper and deeper depression. Before each day ended, he'd again find comfort in alcohol, going to bed drunk. His shattered dream of creating a world-renown addiction clinic plunged him into hopeless despondency. Further sessions with Gus Ginther were wasted time. His jaundiced yellowish skin was symptomatic of a deteriorated liver now close to shutting down forever. Once viewed by townsfolk as a hero, he was now the object of derision by the locals (led by Paige) because he'd reverted to alcoholism.

****

It was the dawn of another perfect late spring day in the mountains of north Georgia. The morning air was a bit chilly, the sky a light powder blue. The sun rising over distant eastern mountains gave promise of lifting daytime temperature into the upper seventies. Shortly after sunrise Tom Owens was out in the garden behind his house.

Tom's only pleasure was his garden. In March it'd been plowed with a neighbor's tractor, a neighbor who'd lived less than a quarter mile to the north, a neighbor who raised cabbage on his small farm in a fertile valley at the base of Sugar Loaf Mountain, a neighbor who made extra cash plowing small spring gardens for a charge of five dollars.

Already, in early June, his long rows of potato plants were at least six inches above ground. Two rows of onion plants were doing well, as were his pole beans that had started climbing up wire cones surrounding each plant. Leafy lettuce was already producing table food for salads. Two rows of lacy green carrot tops defined the garden's west edge.

Tom's morning routine was cultivating his beloved plot of fertile soil before the day became too hot and before his damaged liver forced him to his bed. His double wooden-handled push cultivator was a gift from his late preacher father who also had been an avid gardener. One of Tom's simple pleasures was inhaling the smell of freshly turned earth as he pushed the cultivator up and down each fifty foot row of plants.

It was about eight a.m. Tom was standing at the edge of his garden, leaning on the twin handles of the cultivator, admiring the result of his morning's labor. There was not a weed to be seen. The many rows of green plants were as straight as an arrow. The red earth around each thirsty plant had been freshly turned in anticipation of an afternoon rain shower. It was a form of beauty only a dedicated horticulturist could appreciate.

To the north and about twelve hundred feet above him, was the nearby summit of Sugar Loaf Mountain. Overlooking Tom's garden below, a single bearded sniper lay sprawled belly-down on a flat rock out-cropping. It was the same spot on which he and three other Columbian assassins had perched when they murdered four people on that fateful day three years earlier. For only a few hours on that day, Tom had experienced the proudest moment in his life as he'd witnessed the first graduating class, knowing that twenty-five men and women had conquered their addictions. His Rehab Clinic was a success and was receiving nationwide recognition for its program.

But that was then.

The crosshairs of his custom made sniper's rifle were focused on Tom's chest. This was the same assassin who earlier had missed his target. After U.S. authorities had finally given up their search for the killers, Señor Vanegas sent him back to the States to complete the mission he'd failed: "Kill Tom Owens." The Cartel had spent millions financing the creation of the Owens' Clinic to make it a secret distribution center for Columbian cocaine. By refusing to employ their agent within his clinic, Tom had destroyed their plans. The Cartel neither forgets nor forgives anyone who disobeys them.

Tom's wife was in the kitchen of their house preparing breakfast when she heard a "cracking sound." Glancing out the kitchen window to monitor her husband's safety she was horrified by what she saw. His body was slumped on top of the wooden handles of the tipped over cultivator. Over his chest bright red blood was rapidly soaking through his white sweat shirt, dripping down onto the freshly plowed ground. Cartel-style justice had finally been administered. Tom Owens was dead.

On this day, June 2nd, the folk in Clermont would later learn about three more murders. A fifth would never be solved.

CHAPTER 30
EARLY WEDNESDAY, MORNING,
JUNE 2, 1971

When Vera Owens saw her husband bleeding profusely out in the garden, before rushing to him, she instantly picked up the kitchen phone, dialed the emergency EMS number pasted on the phone's base. Quickly giving them her address and crisis situation, she hung up, rushed out into the garden. With her training as an anesthesiologist she tried to stop the bleeding and resuscitate him. All her valiant efforts were in vain. Within ten minutes the paramedics arrived but Tom was dead.

In the Sheriff's office, located in the rear section of the County Court House, all EMS phone calls are monitored. Vera's frantic call prompted Sheriff Howard Lammar to immediately dispatch a police car to the Owens' house. After their arrival the deputies radioed Lammar that his death was a carbon copy of the four murders years earlier, the shot having come from the summit of Sugar Loaf Mountain.

In 1968 the intensive police search had eventually discovered the hideout of the four assassins. However, it was discovered weeks after the quadruple murders. The assassins had long since fled. Lammar kept his discovery of their hideout a secret from the public.

Upon hearing of the death of Tom Owens this twenty-year veteran policeman's instinct immediately kicked in. He ordered the radio dispatcher to contact all police cars out patrolling county roads, instructing them to meet him PDQ at the entrance to Blackberry Mountain Forest Preserve, coming silently, no sirens, with only red/blue lights flashing along the route.

As Lammar's vehicle sped west along State Highway 56, eight other police cars turned off from contiguous side roads and joined the urgent procession. With red/blue lights flashing, sirens silent, they formed an impressive motorcade.

Before leaving the court house Lammar had ordered a SWAT team to assemble and come to the Blackberry hideout where he and the other deputies would have the remote cabin surrounded.

Within one hour after the murder of Tom Owens, the SWAT team arrived. Lammar and his deputies knew someone was obviously hiding within. They knew because of a ten year old battered Dodge pickup truck parked behind it, hidden from an aerial view by the cliff's overhang.

Over a loud speaker Lammar ordered whoever was inside to come out of the door with hands in the air. Lammar was betting the murder of Tom Owens was connected to the triple killing three years earlier. From inside the cabin the response was a single rifle shot that wounded one of his deputies hiding behind a pine tree not quite wide enough to conceal all of him. Lammar ordered two other deputies to carry the wounded officer several hundred yards down the rocky trail, there to be picked up by an EMS crew that always followed the SWAT team.

The person inside the cabin was obviously an expert marksman. The SWAT team, even with their bullet proof shields and flexible body armor, was leery of making a rush on the cabin and its occupant. The confrontation was a standoff.

Lammar ordered his men to prepare to shoot in a pattern that would cover each section of the cabin's exterior: the door, two windows, the wooden siding between the door and windows. At his command they began firing. The mountains echoed and re-echoed with the one minute fusillade of exploding bullets and their lead projectiles penetrating the cabin's exterior.

Lammar ordered the firing to stop. Surely the cabin's occupant had to be either wounded or dead. What they could not know was that their assailant had sought protection from the lethal salvo by crawling up into the cabin's sooty stone fireplace chimney.

As the police waited there was an eerie silence, a sharp contrast to the cacophony of firing guns the previous minute. After a short interval, with the precision of a professional sniper, the explosion of one rifle shot fatally picked off one of Lammar's deputies, Hoyt Cross, who'd carelessly exposed himself because he'd mistakenly assumed the gunman inside had been killed. A rapid second shot wounded another of Lammar's men who'd partially protected himself behind the trunk of a century old pine tree. The SWAT team again unleashed a torrent of fire at the cabin to prevent the crazed trapped marksman inside from shooting the rescuers of the two deputies, one apparently dead and the other seriously wounded.

Four brave policemen risked their lives to drag both deputies to the protection of a large log behind a rhododendron thicket where they quickly applied a tourniquet to the wounded policeman. His wound stabilized, they then supported him down the steep dirt road to a waiting ambulance. Behind them paramedics carried the dead man on a stretcher to the same waiting ambulance that immediately sped off to the distant Clermont Hospital.

Lammar ordered the SWAT team to lob a tear gas shell into the cabin. Seconds later the canister exploded sending a cloud of toxic gas throughout the one-room interior. White fumes could be seen seeping out broken glass windows and from a gap at the bottom of the front door.

Without warning, the assassin suddenly came charging out the door, coughing, tears flowing from red inflamed eyes. His crazed mind dazed and partially blinded he stood erect on the porch indiscriminately firing his automatic rifle into the surrounding terrain, bullets inaccurately whizzing throughout the woods in which the police were hiding.

A marksman from the SWAT team shot the murderous Columbian squarely in the chest. He fell onto the porch's wooden floor, his finger reflexively pulling the trigger of his weapon. Lest he stand up and take aim, another SWAT team deputy shot him in the head.

Within less than a minute his body became motionless. He appeared dead.

Pistol gripped tightly in his hand, its barrel aimed at the downed killer, Sheriff Lammar himself cautiously approached the fallen sniper, and wary he might revive and again begin firing his rifle. Lammar kicked the assassin's gun off the porch and then knelt down to examine the bleeding bearded man to determine if he was in fact dead. He was. Mixed in with the now diluted tear gas seeping out from the cabin's open door was the distinct coppery smell of the assassin's blood oozing from his multiple wounds, an odor Lammar would never forget.

In a search of his clothing there was nothing to determine who he was. Nothing within the sparse furnishings in the cabin led to his identification. Later, however, earlier fingerprints taken from one of the four buried rifles on top of Sugar Loaf Mountain would match his. That was the only knowledge ever gained about him. His body, after lying two months in the corner's morgue, remained unclaimed. It was buried in an unmarked grave in the corner of a local County cemetery, the place reserved for the dead bodies of anonymous prisoners.

No one in Clermont was ever aware of the connection between Tom Owens and this unidentified killer, or this killer's connection to the Drug Cartel in Bogotá, Columbia.

Gus Ginther, because of his therapy sessions with Tom, could have provided vital information, but before the day ended he would not be alive to testify about what he knew.

The F.B.I. was suspicious of Tom Owens and his years living in Bogotá. Its agents were close to discovering the connection between Tom Owens' and the Columbia Drug Cartel. However, with his death the trail quickly became cold.

Doctor Paige when interviewed by FBI agents back on September 21, 1968, the day of the Saturday massacre, thought he knew about the Cartel connection to the Owens' Clinic. FBI agents concluded, however, that without evidence, Paige's so-called knowledge was only the result of a paranoid mind. They never discovered his perfidious role in securing the assassin's remote hideout.

Now years later, on a Wednesday, June 2, 1971, three more people would be murdered.

Clermont County would never again be the same. For its citizens their fear of strangers would be intensified.

CHAPTER 31
NOON, WEDNESDAY,
JUNE 2, 1971

"Hello Peggy. What a pleasant surprise to see you. I was just preparing to have my midmorning cup of tea. Come in and share a pot of tea with me, so...."

"No, Doris. Thanks anyway. I need to find your husband."

"He always takes Wednesday off...so..."

"Oh, I'd forgotten that today's his day off."

"So tell me, why did you need to see Henry? So is something...."

Doris Paige never completed a sentence, always connecting thoughts with the conjunction "so." Peggy wondered if that was because she had a dominating husband like Henry Paige who, when in any group, always monopolized the conversation. Henry Paige had a "god complex." Because he was a doctor he therefore thought he knew everything about everything. When her husband was not present Doris was reluctant to relinquish her domination in any dialogue.

Interrupting Doris, Peggy said, "I've applied for an insurance policy and they want my doctor's signature on the health section of the application. If I don't mail it today I'll miss the discount they offer."

"Well Henry has forbidden any patient from bothering him when he's out at our lake house, so...."

"I'll not bother him out at his lake house. I'll come to his office at the clinic tomorrow and have him sign it. He can post date his signature and the insurance company will not know the difference between today's date and tomorrow's."

"Can't you come in and join me in a cup of tea, or coffee, and some cookies? I'd like to get to know you, the wife of the man my husband dislikes so much. Just because our husbands are enemies doesn't mean we must dislike each other. Besides, we're both part of the Woman's Aid Society at our church. Don't you just adore our new preacher? So...."

Peggy Gist again interrupted Doris by repeating what she'd just uttered so Doris would hopefully later remember what she'd said, "Well tomorrow...." She emphasized that word. "...tomorrow I'll go to his office for his signature. I don't want to bother him at his lake house on his day off. Now I'll go back home." Peggy's motive for what she'd planned overruled truth. Her entire life was a lie: hiding her infectious disease, concealing her sexual preference for women. She was good at being deceitful. She also guessed that Paige's naïve wife was unaware of her husband's amorous relationship to his nurse, Gretchen.

Doris was such a wimp. All she cared about was the status of being the wife of the town's most beloved physician. She was president of the town's Garden Club, chairperson for the town's annual Thanksgiving "Feed the Poor" campaign, and a devout worker in several other benevolent community groups. Everyone knew that as the "good doctor's wife" she was flakey, shallow, superficial. But she played the pretend game other prominent wives of powerful men played, pretending she didn't know about marriage infidelities among the wealthy power structure within the community. In Clermont culture, the sin was not committing adultery but admitting adultery.

"The lake moisture hurts my sinuses so.... Henry doesn't even have a telephone out there. That's one reason he likes our lake house so out there he can get away from people calling him, wanting him to doctor them...so... he likes to fish. Just last week he told me about the two big bass he caught. Right now he's probably sitting out on the dock with a fishing pole in his hands. Fishing is his recreational passion... so..."

Peggy knew if she didn't interrupt Doris, she'd never stop talking. "I don't want to bother him today." For the third time she repeated, "I'll go to his office early tomorrow, get his signature then. I'll put today's date on the form. Tomorrow Doctor Paige can put today's date above his signature." She turned, said, "Goodbye. I'm sorry if I interrupted your midmorning tea time." As she began walking down the cement sidewalk she could hear Doris Paige's fading voice behind her. "So...did you know that Henry was awarded....?"

Peggy began trotting toward her car, got in, started the engine and drove away. Her original plan had been if he was at his in-town house she'd lure him to get into her car, drive him up to the State Park on the summit of Sugar Loaf Mountain, entice him to accompany her on a walk out the short mountain trail to the site where the assassins had laid when firing their deadly salvo on the Owens' Clinic. When he wasn't looking, she'd push him off the cliff and to his death. Later she'd claim he'd made sexual advances, they scuffled, in the melee he tripped and fell to the jagged rocks ninety feet below. Since Ginther's recent revelation that she didn't have but a few months to live, she was willing to risk a murder conviction to take revenge for his intentional incorrect diagnosis, the result of Paige's hate for her husband.

Now, however, the voices within her mind told her that with Paige out at his lake house this was her ultimate opportunity. She pointed her automobile toward Lake Nelson, fifteen miles west of Clermont. She reached under the driver's car seat. Yes. Her gun was there.

On the drive to Lake Nelson she was surprised to see so many police cars, both Georgia State Troopers and County Sheriff's cars, speeding around her, obviously rushing to some crime scene on the west side of the county. She sensed this was the perfect time to do what she was planning. It seemed every policeman in north Georgia was hurrying to some destination beyond where she would turn off the main highway onto a smaller road that led to the lake and the doctor's second home.

Arriving about ten thirty at the Paige lake house, she drove around to the back, stopped her car in front of the double garage attached to the house with a covered walkway. After turning off the car's ignition and quietly opening and closing the door she peered through the garage windows and there saw two vehicles. One she recognized as Paige's black Buick Roadmaster sedan. The other, a Chevy station wagon, she recognized as Gretchen Schroeder's.

She walked up and onto the back porch of the elaborate two story hillside house. Peering through the ornate glass door she saw no one but could hear faint laughter coming from the lower level. Soundlessly she tried the door knob, expecting it to be locked. It wasn't. She gently twisted it, opened it. The laughter from the lower ground level grew louder. She descended the muted carpeted stairway to the lower level that opened out onto a patio deck that overlooked the lake. Cautiously, silently, she walked down the carpeted hall toward the source of the voices that were increasing in volume. They were coming from the downstairs bedroom.

"Oh Henry! Oh Henry! You know all the right buttons to press on me." She heard the woman in the bedroom loudly laughing. It was a rapturous orgasmic laugh. "Oooh Henry! Oooooh Henry!"

His loud response was, "Come on baby, light my fire! Come on baby, light my fire!"

Peeking through the partially closed door she saw Paige and Gretchen making love on the huge king sized bed. They were so consumed with their passion that Peggy could have yelled at the top of her voice and the two wouldn't have heard her.

Without delay and disgusted with what she was viewing, Peggy stealthily walked straight to the side of the bed, the pistol tightly gripped in her hand. As a teenager, her father's instructions about how to shoot a pistol were about to pay off.

She pointed the weapon at the back of the head of the good doctor, the man who because of a feud with her husband had intentionally misdiagnosed her illness and thus sentenced her to a humiliating death. Inside her head a loud voice repeatedly screamed, "Shoot the bastard! Shoot the bastard!" At point-blank range she pulled the trigger. A dark hole appeared in his head and instantly a stream of red blood gushed out. The hairy body of the naked pot-bellied fifty-nine year old doctor collapsed on top of his plump naked nurse. The voice inside Peggy's head then yelled, "Kill her!" She pointed the gun at the moaning woman being crushed beneath the doctor's dead weight. Again she pulled the trigger. The bullet entered Gretchen's left temple. Bright red blood spurted out from the fatal wound and onto the white pillow case and bed sheets.

Without waiting to enjoy her moment of revenge, Peggy Gist turned and briskly walked out of the bedroom, up the stairs and out of the house, wiping finger prints off door knobs with the hem of her dress. The voices within her head were complementing her for her successful retaliation. She got into her car, started the engine, pulled the gear handle down to "reverse," slowly backed out of the gravel driveway. No one had seen her arrive. No one saw her leave. Her pistol, now in her purse, was unregistered. Its lethal bullets in the dead bodies couldn't be traced.

She'd committed the perfect crime. She'd lied to Doris Paige about not driving out to the doctor's house on Lake Nelson. A voice inside her head reminded her no one could force her to incriminate herself, reminded her that for the past twenty years she'd successfully lived a lie about her disease, about her past unhappy life in Baltimore. The inner voice told her she was clever and creative and the local police weren't too smart.

The voice within her mind reminded her how fortunate she was to arrive at the exact moment the doctor was preoccupied with making love to his nurse, so preoccupied that he was unaware of anyone entering the bedroom.

As she drove back home, her twisted thoughts drifted into a psychotic realm: *Perhaps, just perhaps, there's a deity of deceit, a divine spirit specializing in guiding the mentally gifted in the circumvention of truth as others conceive of truth. After all, truth isn't absolute but relative, merely a function of the upper limits of the gifted individual's mind to think creatively. What's truth to one person may or may not be truth to someone who has a greater capacity to reason on a higher intellectual level. Perhaps this holy being helps people with incredible astuteness to finesse those less gifted. What one person labels a lie will not be a lie to another person with this superior discernment. Perhaps this god of alleged deceit will soon reveal to me I never actually had syphilis, that I've been lied to by someone who worships this unholy spirit of deception, namely Doctor Paige. Perhaps, just perhaps, because all my life I've always been a successful manipulator of truth, this sovereign will lengthen my life and allow me to live in luxury and good health with the wealth I've inherited. But then, can I trust a deity of deceit?*

With no core values as the foundation of her beliefs, she now wondered about such things. To Peggy Gist such convoluted mental machinations seemed to be evidence of her superior brainpower.

Driving back into town, several times she had to steer her car off to the side of the highway to allow many police cars and ambulances to pass. She wondered what had happened west of town, out near the Blackberry Mountain Forest Preserve.

Just outside of the Clermont City limit sign she pulled her car off into a small grass-covered driveway leading to an old decrepit log house with its roof partially caved in. This historic structure was the frontier homestead of the ancestors of a now wealthy Georgia family living down near Atlanta in an exclusive gated community known as "Stone Mountain." These proud descendants kept their property outside Clermont unchanged as a reminder to their pioneer roots in Clermont County. Behind it was a deep well dug by its 18th century settlers. Mossy partially rotten planks supposedly secured the top of this deep pit but they contained several large jagged openings.

Exiting her auto, Peggy walked over to the century old well, extracted from her purse her pistol, dropped it through the hole in the well's covering. She listened. Two seconds later she heard a faint splash as the gun hit water, then a slight burbling sound as it buried itself in mud at the bottom. No one would ever find it.

It was nearly noon as she drove into the driveway of her house up on a mountain crest overlooking the city of Clermont. She parked her car in the double garage besides her husband's black Cadillac sedan. Entering the house through the door leading into the kitchen she was surprised to see her husband sitting out on the deck, randomly gazing out over about twenty miles of near and distant mountain range shrouded in a light blue haze.

Lying across his lap was his deer hunting 30/30 rifle.

She quickened her footsteps into the kitchen and out the screen door to the attached large wooden deck. She was anxious to report to her husband the success of her mission. The voice inside her head was complimenting her for her completed assignment and curious about whether her husband's task had also been successfully completed.

Chapter 32
Wednesday Evening, June 2, 1971

"What are you doing out here on the deck?" First giving her husband a casual look, then focusing on the rifle lying across his lap, then making direct eye contact she hesitantly added, "Did you use it?"

"No." The single syllable answer had uncertainty within it. He was holding a lit cigar tightly between the first and second fingers of his right hand. With his little finger he dexterously tapped the stogie's end and excess white ash dropped down onto the deck. He placed the cigar between his lips and clenched teeth. His words were slightly distorted as he further added, "If he'd reported us to the State Health Department on Monday my future would've been ruined." This statement was followed by his characteristic mannerism of swinging his hand up to his head and with spread fingers "combing" graying strands of unruly hair.

She eased herself down on the edge of the seat of the wicker chair next to him, leaned in his direction, anxious for details. "Yes. I know that. But did you do what we'd agreed had to be done?"

"I didn't have to. Someone else did it for us." He blew heavy smoke from his cigar up into the air. With the index finger of his right hand he rubbed his nose, then gave her a sideway glance.

Surprised, she asked, "What do you mean?" Before she settled back in the chair she took out a pack of cigarettes, tapped one out, picked up her husband's cigar lighter from the end table, lit the cigarette, slowly blew the smoke up and away from her husband, then turned to face him. "You're saying Ginther is dead but you didn't kill him?"

"Yeah. That's what I'm saying. I was parked on the side of the road, just south of the bridge over Salvation Creek, on that deserted stretch, my car half concealed behind a large clump of mountain laurel. About a quarter mile ahead I saw him approaching, rapidly peddling his bicycle, head bent down over the handle bars, legs moving up and down like a well-oiled machine. I had my rifle pointed out the window, safety off, waiting for him to come up the hill, just a little closer, his head in the cross hairs of my scope. I waited for the right moment so I could take my best shot. Then, out of nowhere someone else shot him! I was stunned! I saw him fall off his bike, saw his body sprawled motionless on the road, blood spurting out from both temples."

Startled, she leaned forward. "Did you see who did shot him?" As the implication of his answer began to sink into her mind she took another drag on her cigarette.

"No. The shot came from somewhere off the western edge of the road, from up in a thick patch of blackberries and rhododendrons." He paused, unsure of what he was about to say, "… somewhere from behind a huge pine tree up on the hillside." He paused, "I'm not really certain exactly where it came from."

"What'd you do?" She settled back in the chair, her face frozen in shock, anxious to hear his answer, again inhaling calming nicotine laden smoke from her cigarette.

"I quickly turned my car around, headed south in case another automobile might come by and incriminate me. With a high-powered rifle in my car I couldn't afford to be identified as being present at the crime scene." With both hands he made a quick motion up to his head, "combing" spread fingers through the hair on both sides of his head.

"You're certain no one saw you leave?"

"Absolutely certain. As usual that old dual lane highway was empty of traffic."

There was a prolonged disconcerting silence between them. Both were trying to determine what this mystery killing meant to them. Finally Peggy, cigarette between her fingers, arose, walked over to the railing outlining the spacious redwood deck of their house, stared off at the distant layered mountain peaks cloaked in their usual blue haze. She finally turned to face him as a hint of a smile appeared on her face. "Are you certain Gus Ginther is dead?"

"No doubt about it. Fifteen minutes later, as I was doubling back into town, now driving on the new expressway parallel and about a quarter mile east from the old highway, I saw a police car speeding on the old highway, its red and blue lights flashing, going south to the place where I'd been, where Ginther lay dead on the road."

She mused, "I wonder who else wanted Ginther dead as much as we did? What was their reason for killing him?" Head bowed, she hesitated, "We can be thankful someone else did it for us. They won't be hunting for us." She placed her cigarette between her lips, inhaled deeply and then exhaled, a long column of smoke coming from both mouth and nostrils. "I liked the man. I wished things could have been different."

"He was okay," he casually replied. "At least we no longer have to worry about him reporting us." He smiled a self-satisfied grin, as he looked at her and said, "You know how strong my sexual urges are. In the past few years I've had dozens of women, both local and in Atlanta." He took a long self-satisfied drag on his cigar, blew the smoke away from where she was seated.

"I know." She also smiled as she pressed her smoldering cigarette butt down in the ash tray on the small table between them. "You know my preference has mostly been with women. It's safer." She added, "We're a perfect team. You can't get enough satisfaction with women." Her words evaporating into the crisp cool evening mountain air, as she quietly added, "... and neither can I." Now totally relaxed she removed another cigarette, lit it, blew smoke up and away from her husband.

There was another lull in their conversation. Both were experiencing an emotional letdown from a very stressful day. Finally, Charles mused, "Anyhow, Ginther's dead. He'll not be able to report our diseases." Then he thought about Paige and his attempted extortion of money from him. Spontaneously he muttered, "Paige, that son-of-a-bitch!" He looked at his wife, shifted his body to the edge of his wicker chair and hesitantly asked, "Did you fulfill your mission? Did you take care of him?"

"It worked out better than I planned." She flashed him a smile. "I drove out to Paige's lake house, caught him and Gretchen in bed really going at it. They never saw me, never even knew I was there. I put a bullet in the back of Paige's head. Before she knew he wasn't making love to her, I put a bullet in her temple. Neither ever saw it coming." She placed her cigarette between her lips, deeply inhaled, simultaneously blew smoke out from both nostrils. She uncrossed her ankles, leaned back in the chair. Back in Clermont I stopped at Paige's office, entered the back door with the key I'd earlier stolen from Gretchen's desk, removed my chart from his file rack, my chart identifying me with syphilis. It's now out in my car. I'll destroy it later this evening after I browse through it."

Having heard his wife's successful report Charles leaned back in his chair, more relaxed. "Perfect. Now it's just the two of us and eight hundred million dollars to give us a life style we've dreamed about." He paused, then poured bourbon into a second crystal glass, handed it to Peggy, picked up his own glass, "Here's to us and 800 million dollars. I knew you were my soul-mate the moment we met years ago in the Clermont Café."

"To us" she replied. They clinked the rims of their glass tumblers. Each took a sip, lowered their glasses, then spontaneously repeating, "To us."

Mild excitement in her voice, Peggy said, "And don't forget the two hundred million inheritance I'll receive when the estate of my parents is settled in a few months. I was their only child."

It was that additional two million that kept him from divorcing her, money he'd inherit after she died in about a year.

Unaware of his thoughts, she again tapped her glass against his, gave him one of her flashing smiles. "To us and our one billion dollars." Her smile was warm and inviting.

"That two hundred million only sweetens our dreams." He then frowned as he recalled Ginther's revelation that he also probably had syphilis. He remembered recent sores in his genitals, sores that hurt when he urinated. He wondered what stage of syphilis he was in. Was he in that third incurable stage as was his wife? He wondered how he could be cured without his infectious disease being reported to health officials. Perhaps they could do as the extortionist Dr. Paige had suggested to him the day before she'd killed him. Perhaps they'd both move to Europe and there begin a new life, there receive the medical cures both needed, and then live happily ever after.

As an attorney, his legal mind-set caused him to wonder what would happen to all his money after his eventual death. He assumed his wife would die before he did. To himself he vowed that later this very evening he'd write his legal will. In his twenty-some years of practicing law he'd made a lot of pocket money writing wills for the distribution of the estates of hundreds of clients so as to minimize the amount the government would take. He knew he'd have to eventually give away what remained of his fortune. Neither he nor his wife had children or relatives. Since the death of his parents two years earlier and since the death of his wife's parents in that tragic airplane crash, he wondered where to bequeath the remainder of his estate after his demise. It would have to be to a tax-exempt organization.

And then in a serendipitous moment of self-inspiration, from somewhere deep within unconscious hereditary memory cells the answer came to him, the perfect recipient for his riches after his death. He couldn't explain this choice. He only knew that the choice gave him a strange sense of satisfaction.

Later that evening he wrote out his last will and testament, placed the document in a wall safe within his house.

Now, sitting on the deck of their mountain top house, there were several minutes of silence between them. Both were reflecting on their physical affliction and their beliefs that what they'd done was justified retaliation for what their victims deserved. As he continued staring off at the distant mountain range, after his decision to write up a will yet this evening, Charles Gist quietly expressed his philosophy about life. "Money is power. Power makes all behavior right. That's my belief."

"Amen," she said, adding, "In this one life we have here on planet Earth, everything is permitted, nothing prohibited. Death is the end of everything. After death there's nothing, no hereafter, no judgment, nothing. That life-after-death crap clergymen rant about is a cruel hoax perpetuated by money-grabbing Bible-thumping religious zealots. Social justice and human mercy are both a religious myth. In the evolutionary progression of life, the strongest and most intelligent survive. The weak and less intelligent don't. While you're alive you get what you can, anyway you can, when you can." She looked over at her husband and flashed him her characteristic smile. His head was nodding in agreement. She concluded, "That's my belief."

He reached for the bottle of brandy as he said, "Amen." He poured another few ounces in his empty glass, took a sip, wiped his lips and repeated, "Amen."

"Our relationship," she said, "to one another is different from those traditional ninnies in that stupid city down there." She pointed to Clermont nestled in the valley below their mountain top home. "We take what we want and have the intelligence to do it successfully." Alien voices within her mind whispered, "Amen."

Attorney Gist nodded approval of his wife's beliefs. He then began grinning as the sweetness of revenge filled his woozy brain. The death of Henry Paige ended their decade old feud and he's won. He picked up the decanter from the table beside his deck chair, refilled his glass, took a long sip, with the back of his hand wiped his lips and muttered, "Ahhhh, life is good."

This moment was a private celebration, the crowning achievement in his and her self-indulgent lives. He mumbled, "One billion dollars, all ours." He took another sip of bourbon, stood up and carefully leaned his rifle against the deck railing.

"How do we spell happy?" she said as she looked at him.

He quickly answered, "M-O-N-E-Y." Both laughed.

Peggy's mood suddenly changed. "If only..." Her voice tapered off.

"If only what?" he asked.

"If only I'd not had that affair when I was eighteen, that affair with that man back in Baltimore." Her voice choked as she added, "If only I'd never given in to his lust, given in to my desires to please a man, I wouldn't have this disease that will soon take my life, at this time in my life when I've gained more money than I ever dreamed I'd have." Her voice softened as her melancholic words tapered off, "...if only."

There was another awkward silence. Neither knew what to say.

Finally he said, "Money buys health. We have money. We can buy a cure for both of us." Something in the tone of his voice betrayed his hypocritical statement. In the secret labyrinths within his mind he believed, he hoped, she'd soon die from the third stage of her fatal disease. He'd then be free to spend his immense wealth in pursuit of a libertine lifestyle he'd always dreamed about.

As she thought about her disease and Paige's intentional misdiagnosis, partly speaking to herself and partly to her husband, she concluded, "His days of practicing medicine have ended."

"Thank God." Those two unthinking words betrayed his so-called atheistic beliefs.

She mentally noted the contravention between his stated disbelief in a divine being and that spontaneous choice of words. She'd always been somewhat contemptuous of his iconoclasm. In her mind he wasn't as logical about his denial of the existence of a God as she was in her belief that human existence was ultimately senseless and useless. She was thinking about a divorce. She no longer needed him. For now, however, she ignored his thoughtless utterance.

"I suppose the local sheriff will turn this county upside down trying to solve the mystery of who murdered Paige and his nurse..." she hesitated before adding, "... and Gus Ginther." She lowered her gaze, rubbed her forehead for several seconds, "I liked him. He knew how to treat a woman."

Her husband's strong voice snapped her back to reality as he added, "There's no way the investigative trail can lead to us." He stood up, strolled over to the edge of the deck of their mountain top home, stared out at the twenty miles of hazy layered mountain ranges. "I never get tired of this view." He slowly turned to face his wife. "I wonder who shot Ginther."

"We'll probably never know," she said.

"Yep," he responded. "We'll probably never know." As he returned to his chair he placed his now stubby cigar into his mouth, inhaled deeply, blew smoke up into the air and watched it slowly vanish. "Yep. Life is good and is gonna get better with all our money."

As she stood up, she crushed what remained of her cigarette in the ash tray on the table. As she gazed down at the red glowing tobacco embers slowly fading into blackness, suddenly the terrifying thought of her impending death overwhelmed her.

She fell onto the deck, her body convulsing, her thoughts spinning out of control.

Her husband saw her fall, stepped over, knelt down and tried to subdue her spastic body motions that were injuring her as her arms, legs and head were banging against the floor. Her dilated pupils told him she was in shock. This was no epileptic of seizure. It seemed to be a major disturbance within her brain.

He dared not call a doctor or take her to an emergency medical unit in any hospital because he feared in her fugue state she might reveal that she'd killed Paige and Schroeder. Within about a minute her body stopped convulsing.

He picked up her limp form, carried her into their bedroom and laid her on the bed. Her lips were moving as if she was trying to tell him something. But she was unable to speak. The fact was she would never again be able to speak. He didn't know that.

After several minutes, she sat up, swung her legs over to the floor. Frightful facial expressions gave him a hint of what was happening within her mind. Reflexively her hand began covering her ears as if to shut out all sounds. In a pine tree just outside the open bedroom window the evening song of a nearby Carolina Wren could be heard. But the sound she was trying to suppress was internal, not external. Her disease was now in its final stage. Its voice had taken control of her thinking. It was a shrieking reverberating voice, echoing and re-echoing within the convoluted folds in her brain inside her skull. It was a condemning voice. She silently screamed, "I want to live! I don't want to die!"

But no one could hear her.

In her stuporous state this mocking raucous voice within her mind was repeating and would continue to repeat over and over again, again and again and again...forever... throughout eternity, "All your beliefs about life were self-contrived fantasy."

****

From that moment Charles Gist knew what he must do to avoid public exposure of his wife's deviant state of mind. Exiting the bedroom, he went to his house office, opened the wall safe, removed his will, passports and American Express high limit credit card. He placed his will in a large envelope which he addressed to his personal attorney down in Atlanta. Through previous consultations he'd know what to do.

He next quickly packed two suitcases, one for himself, the second for his wife. Five hours later both Charles and Peggy Gist were seated in the first class section of a Delta Airline International jet en route to Berlin Germany.

CHAPTER 33
ABOUT ONE MONTH LATER, JULY, 1971

It was Thursday morning, the day the latest edition of the weekly newspaper, *Clermont Clarion,* was distributed in postal mail boxes (for pre-paid subscribers), sold from coin dispensers in front of the three food supermarkets within the Clermont City limits, sold off the counter in most of the rural grocery stores scattered throughout Clermont County, and sold from metal dispensers in front of area restaurants. Today, the newspaper container in front of the Clermont Café was sold out before eight o'clock.

Tables and booths inside the Café were all filled, especially the "liar's table" which normally seated eight. Today twelve patrons were packed around it. Outside on the concrete sidewalk people were standing in line waiting for inside customers to leave. Few, however, were leaving, lingering over their bottomless cups of coffee, excited about four front-page news stories. Buried in back pages two other stories went unnoticed.

The most exciting news was that the Eleventh U.S. Circuit Court of Appeals in Atlanta had, the previous Monday, in an

205

en banc decision, announced the appeal of the Empire State Insurance Corporation to overturn the lower court's decision in Attorney Gist's billion dollar class-action law suit filed two years earlier had been rejected. The Insurance Corporation on advice from their attorneys declined to petition for a *writ of certiorari* to the U.S. Supreme Court. The long drawn-out litigation was finally over!   Information about Attorney Charles Gist's fee was not revealed but everyone assumed the figure was around eight hundred million dollars, one of the highest fees in the history of class action lawsuits. He'd become an instant local and national celebrity.

Local newspaper reporters wanted to interview him, but he and his wife had earlier and unexpectedly left Clermont for an extended tour of Europe.

The second stunning front page news story was that Attorney Gist and wife Peggy were, for the purpose of tax reduction, donating thirty-six million dollars for the construction of a new forty-bed hospital on Main Street, after the old structure was razed.

The story also stated that for tax purposes, Charles and Peggy Gist were donating four million to the County to be used to pay off municipal bonds sold by County Commissioners to purchase the Owens' Clinic buildings from the bankrupt Owens estate. Thus tax payers would no longer be paying yearly interest payments on the debt for the hospital's purchase.

A third surprising news story stated that Charles and Peggy Gist had announced their intention to purchase the forty acre Tom Owens' Addiction Clinic campus, again for tax reduction purposes. They were donating its buildings and campus to a benevolent organization for the poor and homeless. It was to become a retirement village for indigent County residents. The Gist Foundation had heavily endowed it with forty million dollars so elderly low-income "locals" could live the remaining years of their lives with the best in housing, nourishing meals and medical care.

A fourth front page newspaper story announced that the Gist Foundation had requested that the County Commissioners name the new downtown hospital, "The Doctor Henry Bartram Paige Memorial Hospital" to honor the doctor who had "unselfishly served the health needs of the citizens of Clermont so faithfully for thirty-one years." When construction was completed they stipulated that his faithful wife "Doris" be given the honor of formally dedicating the new building.

No one ever figured out that all the benevolence of Charles and Peggy Gist was done to deflect the police murder investigation away from them.

On page six of the local newspaper, Sheriff Lammars announced that the reward for information leading to the conviction of the murderer(s) of Dr. Paige and his nurse had been increased to two hundred thousand dollars, thanks again to the largesse of the Gist Foundation. The newspaper repeated the circumstances of their murder about how the good doctor and his nurse were at his lake house organizing patient charts when the EMS medics found their murdered bodies.

There was no mention in the newspaper about the persistent rumor that EMS medics upon arrival at the Paige lake house found both the good Doctor and his nurse naked in bed, locked together in love's embrace. The minister of the Methodist Church, the church where Paige was a member in good standing, often preached fiery sermons about the sin of gossip. However, the rumor persisted, fueled by two EMS medics who were deacons in the larger Baptist Church, the Methodist's chief rival for new members.

On the back page of the front section of the *Clermont Clarion,* was a report from Sheriff Lammars that he continued to seek evidence about the tragic murder of Doctor

Gus Ginther. The story repeated that Lammar believed the murderer was a "local." As he'd done so many times in past years, he again requested information that would lead to the conviction of Ginther's killer. He announced that the reward for information leading to the conviction of Dr. Ginther's killer had been upped to two hundred thousand dollars, thanks to a generous donation from the Gist Foundation.

In the *Clermont Clarion*, on the page where obituaries were printed, few people noticed or cared that Maggie Stratton, long time waitress at the Clermont Café, three times divorced, single mother of three boys, had committed suicide. Her close church friends were shocked and had no explanation for her sad act of self destruction. What was not made public was the fact she was six months pregnant. The Georgia medical examiner determined that Maggie had syphilis and her unborn fetus had congenital syphilis. State health detectives were stymied in their attempts to find the source of her contagious disease.

****

So, life in Clermont County returned to the way it had been twenty-five years earlier and especially after that fateful day, June 2, 1971, when six people were murdered, four in seemingly unrelated circumstances. Only two were solved, that of the crazed killer of Tom Owens and Sheriff's deputy Hoyt Cross in the shoot-out at the abandoned hunter's cabin deep within the Blackberry Mountain Forrest Reserve.

The battle over hospitals ended.

Descendants from eighteenth century pioneer settlers in Clermont County, the "old timers" who owned most of the businesses on Main Street, continued giving discounts to "locals" and charging tourists "from off" a ten percent higher price. Realtors continued advising new out-of-state house buyers to change their automobile license tags to Georgia plates as soon as possible to avoid being identified as outsiders. Newcomers who purchased expensive homes in scenic Clermont County were welcome to spend money in Clermont County, but not welcome to get involved in local politics. The court house remained solidly in control of the "locals," all "Yellow Dog Democrats." *(The phrase "Yellow Dog Democrat" originated in the 1870's after the "War Between the States" when on any election day Southerners, out of hate for Republican President Lincoln who'd freed the slaves, would say, 'I'd vote for a yellow dog before I'd vote for a damn Republican.)*

EPILOGUE
JUNE 10, 1971

While traveling south from Berlin, Germany at a high rate of speed in their Mercedes-Benz on German Autobahn A14, both Charles Gist and his invalid wife Peggy were killed in a fiery auto accident at the dangerous intersection of A9, a few kilometers northeast of Leipzig. The local newspaper, *Leipziger Volkszeitung* announced they were rushing for an appointment with a famed epidemiologist for treatment of undisclosed health problems at the world renowned medical center in Leipzig.

Their mutilated and charred bodies were immediately cremated, their ashes placed in two cardboard urns and returned to north Georgia. In a chartered airplane Clermont funeral director George Hamilton directed the pilot to fly over the Blackberry Mountain Forest Preserve where without ceremony their ashes were scattered by the wind and slowly drifted down to settle upon virgin trees and bushes in this remote century old forest.

When the last will and testament of Charles Gist was probated it stipulated that after designated bequests were distributed by the Gist Foundation and all taxes paid, the remainder of his estate should be given to the endowment fund of the North Georgia Sequoyah Boarding School. This K-12 academic institution was for gifted children of parents living in the top eight counties in northern Georgia, and for gifted children living in the nearby Cherokee Reservation in southwestern North Carolina. Administrators of the Gist estate estimated the total bequest to be over 500 million dollars.

Sequoyah, after whom the school was named, was born in Eastern Tennessee in 1776. While yet a small child his parents moved to north Georgia. In 1809, twenty-seven years before the U.S. government forced the Cherokees to leave their land, Sequoyah as a young man formulated eighty-six written symbols that represented all the vocal sounds in the spoken Cherokee language. Prior to Sequoyah's invention of a Cherokee alphabet no Cherokee had ever been able to read or write in their own language. Because of Sequoyah's marvelous creation within a decade his people were able to print and read a Cherokee newspaper, *The Phoenix*, published in New Echota, Georgia. Many books including the Bible were printed in their own language. Sequoyah was the only known person in the history of mankind to invent a complete alphabet without being able to read or write any language other than that spoken by his own race. In the opinion of later university scholars, he was the most remarkable man to have ever lived on Georgia soil

The parents of Charles Gist had a secret no one in Clermont County ever learned, a family secret passed down by their parents who in turn had been taught the secret by their parents. It was a belief in a fact they considered shameful, a shame that to a large degree had shaped their generational behavior. It was the fact that their great great grandfather, a Caucasian fur trader named Nathaniel Gist had, in about 1775, married a "Cherokee squaw," as they contemptuously referred to her. Because of their humiliation over this racist belief they never bothered to learn her name.

Her name was "Wut-teh." Nathaniel and Wut-teh had several sons, one of whom was the intellectual giant named Sequoyah!

Charles Gist was in fact a direct descendant from the gene pool which included the greatest man to ever live in Georgia. Except for those few unexplainable moments when late in his life he wrote his will, Charles Gist was ashamed of this ancestry of which he should have been very proud.

Bad beliefs, bad behavior!

****

In the remote wilderness region adjacent to the Blackberry Mountain Forest Preserve, in the grassy lawn outside a primitive cabin, Chester Howell carried a blue rhododendron blossom picked from a nearby bush. Reverently he placed it on a small granite stone that identified it as a grave. On the stone, in black paint, were the crudely printed words, "ole Blu."

Kneeling beside that simple burial monument, Chester Howell brushed from its flat top a previously placed now brown withered mountain laurel blossom, replacing it with a fresh red flower. He repeated words so often said in past months, "'Ole Blu, I miss you. Besides Doctor Paige, you was the bestest friend I ever had. That new stranger doctor "from off" had no right to shoot you, but I done got us even. I killed him like he done killed you."

END OF STORY